Praise for *Life's Gc*

"Nâzım Hikmet's novel *Life's Good, Brother* is one of the first and most important 'European' novels written in Turkey: its horizons are not limited to the national issues of Turkey, it explores the basic values of life, and its heroes live cosmopolitan lives . . . the narrative progresses by jumps in time and place, sometimes with easy backward glances and sometimes via Dadaist cut-and-paste techniques. . . . The cumulative effect on the reader of these impressions—fixed in simple language and short sentences, these brush strokes—is that of a great lyric poem from the pen of a poet in the throes of the pain aroused by the beauty of life. . . ." —Orhan Pamuk, *Radikal* (Istanbul)

"A written gift of memory and experience. . . . The personal reflections are humorous, the experimental delivery is exciting, and the drama is always profound. One would be hard pressed to find a similar personal reflection on the printed page that reaches such poetic heights."
—James Burt, *ForeWord Reviews*

"Initially published in Turkey in 1964, this novel by one of the country's greatest poets portrays a chaotic time between wars in justifiably haphazard fashion . . . [includes] many graceful gems. . . ."
—*Publishers Weekly*

"Hikmet's commitment to accessibility ensures that the novel is never obscure or confusing, despite sparingly shifting between first- and third-person narration . . . like cutting from medium-shot to close-up or vice versa, that alters our emotional perspective on the characters."
—Ray Olson, *Booklist*

Life's Good, Brother

NAZIM HIKMET
Life's Good, Brother
....

A NOVEL

TRANSLATED FROM THE TURKISH BY
MUTLU KONUK BLASING

A KAREN AND MICHAEL BRAZILLER BOOK
PERSEA BOOKS / NEW YORK

Persea Books, Inc.
277 Broadway, Suite 708
New York, New York 10007

ISBN: 978-0-89255-418-8

Library of Congress Cataloging-in-Publication Data
Nâzım Hikmet, 1902-1963.
[Yasamak güzel sey be kardesim. English]
Life's good, brother : a novel / Nazım Hikmet ; translated from the Turkish by Mutlu Konuk Blasing.— 1st ed.
      p. cm.
"A Karen and Michael Braziller book."
ISBN 978-0-89255-418-8 (alk. paper)
1. Nâzım Hikmet, 1902-1963—Fiction. 2. Authors, Turkish—Fiction. 3. Izmir (Turkey)—Fiction. I. Blasing, Mutlu Konuk, 1944- II. Title.
PL248.H45Y313 2013
894'.3533—dc23
                    2012026329

Designed by Rita Lascaro
Printed and bound by Maple Press, York, Pennsylvania

First Edition

Contents

Introduction
ix

Life's Good, Brother
3

Glossary
189

About the Author
191

Introduction

NÂZIM HIKMET was notorious for his weak memory. "For me," he claimed, "there's no yesterday, only tomorrow." His amnesiac mode, partly willed, was a kind of self-defense: "The weakness of my memory, or sometimes even its total absence, protects me from the nightmare of memories." Yet *Life's Good, Brother*, his last book, written in exile in 1962, is an autobiographical novel steeped in memory. Set in 1925 in Izmir, Turkey, the novel flashes back to Nâzim's earlier years in Turkey and Russia and forward to his then-future years and experiences to come in Turkish detention centers and prisons. Past, present, and future have porous borders in this book that fashions Nâzim's life story as a novel. Even for this most determinedly materialist poet, in the end it turned out that, in James Merrill's words, "life was fiction in disguise."

Edmund White, discussing Jean Genet's *Prisoner of Love*, identifies a sub-genre of late memoirs, where "the memories and experiences of the narrator . . . unfold in a dream-like manner. Sometimes the story starts at the middle or even the end. . . . The text still makes sense, but the leaps from one sentence to another are sometimes perilous." This account of the fluidity of Genet's memory and narrative could just as well be describing Nâzim's autobiographical novel, which also tests the borders between memoir and fiction.

Nâzim introduces another kind of fluidity by deploying a cast of characters to simultaneously tell one man's story and the history of a generation. Ahmet, the main character in the novel, represents many aspects of Nâzim himself. The two share biographical details, and the story of Ahmet easily shuttles between third- and first-person narration, often more than once in a single paragraph. The author/narrator moves in and out of the consciousness of Ahmet, the Communist Party member with a mission to set up an underground printing press in Izmir, and an "I" who meanders through his memories. The remembered and remembering "I" is also a figure of memory, a metaphorical bridge between Ahmet in 1925 and Nâzım in 1962, whose past is Ahmet's future. The first-person pronoun indicates less a here-and-now presence than a fictional entity; essentially nowhere, the "I" works as a switchboard between different times and places.

The stories of Ahmet and Nâzım are both pressured by real-time limits. In Nâzım's case, the limit was his looming death; in the novel, the time limit is set by the threat of rabies as Ahmet, bitten by a possibly rabid dog, keeps anxious count of the forty days of the incubation period by chalking lines on the wooden door of the stone cottage where he is hiding out. This was one kind of prison, a cell corresponding to other stone cells to come, where he would also count his days in the dark with lines scratched on walls.

While the story transpires in 1925, the device of fluid narration interleaves the current events during Ahmet's hiding out in Izmir and the events Ahmet remembers from his earlier years, going back both to his childhood in Istanbul before the First World War and to the heady years of 1921–1924, when he was a student in Moscow. But the 1925-present of the story is also itself the past—recollected by the author in 1962, when he was in exile in a very different Moscow—and this tension necessarily inflects the narrative and the emotional texture of both Nâzım's flashbacks and his forward flashes to experiences Ahmet has yet to live through. Such narrative dissonance serves to maintain a virtual future—in principle, an open future—within an autobiographical and historical past. It redeems the real "time lost," which was not only the past but also the future.

Nâzım lived through several incarnations of both Turkey and Russia in the course of one lifetime. He maintains "what might have been" and "what has been" as equally real or equally unreal; his "time present" and "time past" are both contained in "time future," just as "time future" is contained in "time past." Taken from lines that begin T. S. Eliot's *Four Quartets,* these conceptions of time have different ends, but they pertain to the way Nâzım structures his novel as well as to the historical import of his story. Early, idealistic communism "remains," in Yevgeny Yevtushenko's words, "an inalienable part of history." Belief in a future that did not happen remains an indelible chapter of history nonetheless; it has a compelling authenticity and a very real effect on shaping individual and social experience.

Nâzım and his main character form a similar triangle. Nâzım, the writer (1962), screens himself behind *two* Ahmets—the one in Moscow (1921–24), and the other hiding out in the stone cottage in Izmir (1925)—as he interweaves their stories. This threesome, like the three times and tenses of the book, also has open borders, with several crossings and re-entry points heading in various directions.

Ahmet shares the stone cottage in Izmir with his comrade Ismail. "In Ismail," Nâzım remarked, "there are militants I know, and there's also me." The story of Ismail, a composite of different militants and prisoners, intersects with Nâzım's story intermittently, in a jagged way. Ismail and Ahmet are both Nâzım's "guests," and his hosting "I" positions the other characters in the book to represent the different aspects of his life—his many lives. Ismail's prison experiences and, certainly, his being locked up in the latrine of a naval ship document Nâzım's life. The scenes of physical torture in the book, however, do not reflect Nâzım's personal experience but represent collective experience. The third-person narration that governs Ismail's story when he and Ahmet are together keeps Ismail at a distance from the reader, while the narration of Ahmet's story easily shifts to first-person in the scenes the two share, to offer access to Ahmet's inner world.

The novel has a small cast of characters, and, as in a low-budget movie, the same actors play different parts in Nâzım's life. This fascinating technique of redistributing a self disperses the autobiographical "I" among fictional characters that are amalgams of different sides not only of Nâzım but also of the various life stories of people he knew. Not exactly a *roman à clef* but a complicated version of it, *Life's Good, Brother* becomes something of a historical puzzle, where characters exist independently yet share parts of themselves and the details of their historical experiences with everyone else. Nâzım's technique enables him to speak at once of one man and a generation, without resorting to allegory. If autobiographies mean to make a life story cohere, Nâzım's novel and its broken stories also mean to make a generation's story cohere.

Nâzım as poet never directly appears in this book until the last, short chapter titled "My Guests," where the speaking "I" lists the characters whose stories he has told and reads a poem he wrote—which is a poem by Nâzım Hikmet. Keeping the poet off-stage, out of the story of his political struggle, underlines the difficult relationship between Nâzım's poetic and political commitments. Throughout the book, Ahmet is haunted by two lines of poetry: "The ship with a hundred masts, where is the port it sails for?" and "Listen to the flute's lament, it grieves its separation." The lines voice the longings that underwrite his political commitment, and they work as refrains in the novel. Indeed, Nâzım casts the whole novel as a poem: twenty out of the twenty-six chapters are titled "lines," as if his whole life were a poem in disguise, composed of so many lines inscribed on different walls and doors at different times and in different places. And, as in a poem, the lines of yearning and the lines marking constraints "rhyme."

The 1925 experience in the stone cottage in Izmir, into which the militant Ahmet/Nâzım locks himself, remains confusing in 1962, even after so many decades. It resists retrospective assimilation, even after Nâzım has traveled the whole long road and affirms, in the end, "if I could / begin this journey all over again, / I would." The stone cottage is one kind of prison, and its relationship to other kinds of stone cells is complicated. In the end, the novel seems to say, there is little difference between locking oneself up in a one-room stone cottage for weeks, working to dig a hole in the ground for a literally "underground" press—a hole Ahmet himself likens to his grave—and being locked up in solitary for weeks for such "underground" activities, which in this novel yield nothing more than an empty hole in the ground.

Life's Good, Brother was published posthumously in 1964 in Russian translation; it came out the same year in Paris in a French translation by Münevver Andaç, Nâzım's wife at the time he left Turkey. It first appeared in Turkish, also in 1964, in Bulgaria and was subsequently published in Turkey in 1967. Since then, the novel has been translated into more than fifteen languages, from German, Italian, and Greek to Japanese, Arabic, and Persian. In this translation, I have followed the latest edition from Yapı Kredi Yayınları (2002); I have also restored some passages from earlier editions published in Turkey and, in one case, a passage from the French translation of the novel. My goal has been to present the most complete text available to me. I am grateful to Randy Blasing, who gave this novel the once-over more than once, for his indispensable help in making it available in English now for the first time.

MUTLU KONUK BLASING

Life's Good, Brother

The Beginning

The servant girl led the way and Ahmet followed. They entered the courtyard. It was big, dark, and cool. But why does this girl walk on tiptoes? Is someone sick in the house? Then, before I know it, I'm walking like her, damn it, as if afraid of waking someone. Ahmet started clacking his metal heeltaps. Just to make a point.

They entered a huge hall, even gloomier than the courtyard.

"The bey said to wait here. They're eating."

Ahmet sat down in one of the oversized, linen-covered armchairs. I know what's under the covers: gilded carvings, red velvet. As in my grandfather's seaside house in Üsküdar.

The wall on the right is isinglass; the dining rooms are behind it. And I'm ravenous. The clicking knives and forks whetted Ahmet's hunger more than the aromas of food. Across from him stood a console, a walnut console with one, two, three, four, five drawers. I squint, then open my eyes wide in its mirror. I scratch my nose. I keep pulling at my mustache—if I said it was silky, would I be boasting? Damn it.

"Ahmet Bey, delighted to see you, son."

Ahmet stood up. "Likewise, Uncle."

Şükrü Bey was tall, slim, and gray.

Ahmet and his uncle had last seen each other about two years ago, in Moscow, in the winter of 1923. Şükrü Bey had come to Moscow on rug business when he was arrested, who knows why. He told them he was a close relative of Ahmet, then a student at Eastern Workers' University. One night about seven, Ahmet got a call from the secret police. Yes, he's my relative, I said. Yes, he is one of the Young Turks. But he's not an agent. I don't think so. I can vouch for him. An hour later they brought Şükrü Bey to Ahmet's room. I had borrowed around and set up a first-rate table—everything from black caviar to vodka. Şükrü Bey likes his food and drink. "Ahmet Bey, son," he says, "I will not forget your kindness till the day I die."

"How are you, dear Ahmet?"

"I'm fine, Aunt, thanks."

Aunt Cemile was still beautiful. If the Devil were female, and beautiful—her beauty was like that.

I was in love with Aunt Cemile when I was a child. She still talks about the steam bath in my grandfather's house in Üsküdar and how she trapped me, when I was about three, between her legs and gave me my bath, and I still blush.

Şükrü Bey cleared his throat: "I hope you don't mind, Ahmet Bey, if I ask what brings you to Izmir."

"I thought I could find work here, Uncle. Something I can do. Any work. There's no work to be had in Istanbul now."

Şükrü Bey cleared his throat. I knew what he was going to say. "Truly, Ahmet Bey, my son, I have not forgotten your kindness."

Then he did something I did not expect. He walked up to the window on the right, motioned me to come close, and slightly parted the drawn drapes. Through the branches of the sunlit magnolia tree, over the garden walls, I could see the street.

"See that guy squatting on the corner across the street? The beggar. The bastard is a cop. I'm under surveillance, Ahmet. They won't leave your uncle alone. I have nothing to do with politics any more, but they're still after me. Go back to Istanbul, son. Let things settle down a bit; I'll send you word. If you don't have return money, I'll give it to you. I owe you from Moscow."

"I have money."

"Did they ban your newspapers?"

"Yes."

"Did the arrests start?"

"Not yet"

"The police here would have your photograph."

"I don't think so."

"They would, they would. If they hear you came to see me, we'll both be wasted. They'll arrest your people, too, they will. And me, too. And they'll hand me over to the Independence Tribunal. They will. They will. The Kurdish rebellion is only a pretext—a pretext Mustafa Kemal found to bring back the Independence Tribunals, to bring Ismet back to the Ministry, his man himself and the most merciless. He will take advantage of this situation to avenge himself on the past, on those of us who remain faithful to the Young Turks. Why? Because in the past, when he belonged to the Party, he was not granted the position he wanted. Yes, that's politics. These renegades become the worst enemies of their old party. He will have me arrested, Mustafa Kemal, yes—he's waiting for me to make a wrong move, just one move."

Outside, the sun was dazzling. Ahmet turned left so he wouldn't pass the beggar on the corner. Was he really a cop? Or did Şükrü Bey make up that story to get rid of me?

He started downhill. This wealthy quarter of Izmir, with its closed shutters, magnolia trees, and red-tile roofs, was abandoned to the heat of the sun. And across the way, down below, lay Izmir Bay—wide, calm, closed off. Where do you enter this bay? Where do you exit to the open sea? In 1919 the Greek navy anchored in these waters. The Greek army stepped onto Anatolian soil on these shores, by order of the British, and in the heat of 1922, after the barley harvest and before the wheat, they were driven into the sea from these shores, leaving a burning city behind them. From up here you can see burnt-out black holes, random empty spaces throughout the city. Ahmet saw the first cavalryman who entered Izmir through the flames. For some reason, just a lone horseman; for some reason, a horseman from an Adana village. Why Adana? A red flag in one hand, a bare sword in the other, the Adana horseman who first entered Izmir in 1922. Where is he now, in 1925? What's he doing? Working on which big landowner's farm? A sharecropper? And the Greek Communists? Not those who faced firing squads for inciting the Greek army to revolt—they're buried on Anatolian soil, along with the Mehmets—but the ones thrown in jail? Are they still behind bars on some Greek island?

Ahmet walked down the hill. Below, back of the strand, he went into a coffeehouse. He ordered cheese, a bagel, tea, and a hookah. I told my folks Şükrü Bey would brush me off. But no, you must go see him, they said. Your uncle will find you a job. He did. You must make full use of all legal means. We did. I just hope our uncle Şükrü Bey doesn't inform the police about me. He ordered more cheese. And another bagel. They didn't even ask me to dinner. He had another glass of tea when the waiter brought his hookah. He'll tell the police. He'll phone. If they're putting pressure on the Young Turks, Şükrü Bey would surely be at the top of their list.

Ahmet had smoked hookah only twice in his life, in Istanbul. They say Izmir's hookahs hit you hard if you're not used to them. And that's what happened. His head was spinning. He closed his eyes. A sunlit straw-gold filled his darkness. Hello, Anushka. He felt a pain pierce the left side of his chest like a knife. He opened his eyes. Goodbye, Anushka. A man walked in. He looked around as if searching for someone. He sat at the table on the left. Under his heavy, swollen, half-closed eyelids, he's watching me. He finished his coffee and left. I almost asked the waiter who the man was who'd just left that table.

Ahmet left the coffeehouse. It was late afternoon, but the pavements of Izmir still steamed from the noonday heat.

Ahmet suddenly faced the sea, empty across a burnt-out field. The burnt field is also empty. And here I am, bare-naked, out in the open. They're watching me.

He turned into a back street and entered a neighborhood mosque. The rotting straw mats smelled greasy. By the pulpit a young man in tatters, blind in both eyes, rocked on his knees, reciting the Koran. His bare feet were clean, his soles calloused. Ahmet sat down and leaned back against the wall.

When he was a baby, his grandfather used to put him to sleep reciting Rumi's poetry instead of lullabies.

After I left boarding school—there, we had to perform our prayers and fast—I stopped praying and fasting. And I could never really read the Koran. With its different vowel markings and gemination marks, it all confused me instead of helping. But I was religious. I mean, it hadn't occurred to me that God might not exist. Then one day I thought not about the existence of God but about the religious man: he does good because he expects to be rewarded by God, to go to heaven and enjoy life immortal, and he avoids sin for fear of the punishments of hell. This bondage, this egotism of the religious man, amazed me, as if I had never been religious.

Since that day, Ahmet tried to do everything without fretting about rewards or fearing punishment. One of the reasons I slipped so easily out of God's grasp is that in Anatolia I saw the man of religion at work. This man was not like my Sufi grandfather, or our boarding school's religion teacher in his suit and tie, or even the jovial imam of our neighborhood mosque in Üsküdar. This man, like the ogres in fairy tales, had settled at the fountainhead and cut off the water supply. Over him ruled superstition, hypocrisy, and intolerance—a dark banner of terror.

Resting his head against the wall, Ahmet slept. When he woke, he checked his watch. It had grown dark inside the mosque. Three old men walked in. Maybe it was their white beards, or maybe their incredibly patched sweaters, but they all looked alike, as if they were triplets. The blind *hafız* was still reciting the Koran. And I feel sad. Damn it. "Listen to the flute's lament, it grieves its separation."

Ahmet walked out. He paused under the lamplight at the gate of the mosque's yard. Somebody sat on the threshold. He looks like the beggar Şükrü Bey had pointed out. But maybe not. Obviously, I've been followed. He walked past the beggar. So Şükrü Bey, as soon as I left . . . But maybe Şükrü Bey didn't report me, and the guy just started to shadow me on his own. This morning Ismail had clearly described their meeting place tonight. Ahmet felt the man was right behind him. He'd be an ass to turn and look. He was enraged his heart pounded so hard. He suddenly stopped at the corner and turned around: nobody there. The little lights from houses, filtered through latticework, doubled the desolation of the streets. He turned left.

Either I shook the bastard, or I'm just paranoid. Damn it.

His hand cupping his cigarette, Ismail sat on the bottom step of a ruined stone staircase. They started walking. The moon rose. The narrow street meandered its solitary way among the weathered wooden houses with overhanging covered balconies. Such silence, such loneliness. I'm a tiny fish. I had this feeling once before, on another moonlit night when I stepped off a dark train and walked around Harkov, a city I didn't know. The two left the city. The moonlit silence now throbbed with the deep *dum-dum* of a motor. I got anxious. We were walking on a dusty road. Nothing to be seen—no trees or houses. We came to the foot of a bare hill on the right. The motor was now roaring. On the slope of the hill stood a lone stone cottage. No windows.

"What's with this motor, Ismail?"

"They're pumping water night and day. It's an hour away."

Ismail unlocked the big padlock on the wooden door of the cottage. He lit the gas lamp. Ahmet sat down on one of the two cots.

"It's as if you knew I was coming."

"The cot is left over from Ziya."

The floor was dirt. Ismail spread out bread, white cheese, tomatoes, and cucumbers from the food cupboard and brought salt and a bottle of water.

"Are you sure we weren't followed, Ismail?"

"These guys aren't spirits, brother—we'd have sensed them."

Ahmet got up, still crunching his cucumber. He stomped his feet on the floor. "I just hope it isn't rock under here."

"Why would it be rock? I have the axes and shovels left over from Ziya. Wood, saws—whatever you need, I'll get."

"No one knows I'm staying with you, right, Ismail?"

"I haven't even told anyone you're in town." Ismail slowly started undressing. "I'll get your suitcase from the station; it's best if you aren't seen around town." He was left in his cotton underpants, tied at the ankles, and his undershirt with missing buttons. His big, dark, strong hands stood out all the more.

Ahmet again tapped the floor with his foot. "Tomorrow I'll measure this and draw up a plan."

"I think the depth and width shouldn't be less than two-and-a-half meters. And you can do a charcoal sketch of it."

"Is your factory far from here, Ismail?"

"About an hour. I wake up at dawn."

He was setting an alarm clock with a bell bigger than the clock. It was also left over from Ziya. He stuck the clock under his pillow. "So it won't wake you."

Ahmet started to undress. Ismail pulled his blanket up to his chin.

"You'll find tea, sugar, and stuff in the cupboard. And the kerosene burner is in the corner. Left over from Ziya. Now blow out the lamp."

"Should I close the door?"

"If you can sleep in the moonlight, leave it open; we'll get some air. Ziya couldn't."

Ahmet had stripped to his boxers and T-shirt. The rough pile of his blanket prickled Ismail's chin. Thirteen years later, in 1938, in the Ankara military prison they would throw him in solitary for six months. Solitary was a stone cell. A window with iron bars but no glass. Snow blew inside. And the floor was concrete.

Ismail would remember this night—how the blanket prickled his chin, how Ahmet kept trying but couldn't blow out the lamp.

"Ahmet, just turn down the wick."

Ahmet didn't but still blew out the lamp.

Moonlight streamed through the open door. Ismail started snoring lightly. And the motor went *dum-dum-da-dum-dum*.

Ahmet tossed and turned, closing his eyes tight and then opening them. He sat up in bed. The moon lit up his face. And the motor went *dum-dum-da-dum-dum*. In Üsküdar, in the house by the sea, I would sit up in bed, my insides wrenched, listening to the rumble of motorboats grinding into the night on their endless journeys.

Ahmet got up and took the pack of cigarettes and matches from his pants draped over the wicker chair. The gun almost fell out of his back pocket. I don't even know how to shoot this thing, but I still carry it around. Damn it. He sat on the threshold and lit his cigarette. The road below, following its lonesome way, shuddered with the throbbing of the motor.

From where I sat, now and then I raised my head to look at the girl across from me, peeling potatoes like me. It's almost noon. Outside, it's snowing in Moscow, but the university kitchen is nice and warm. Why won't the girl across from me take off the shawl covering her head and shoulders? On my left is my Political Economy professor; on my right, Hüseyinzade, an Iranian student; next to him is Si-Ya-U, a Chinese student; beside him is the spongecake wife—too many eggs and too much baking soda—of the university rector; next to her, someone I don't know, but from his nose I'd guess he's Russian; next to him is the blue-eyed girl I keep raising my eyes to look at; next to her is Petrosian, a Red Flag Medal pinned on the shirt buttoned up to his neck—he's the secretary of the university Party cell. We're all seated on wooden benches around a huge bucket, on KP.

We pick the potatoes out of the sacks—one more gnarled and muddier than the other, damn it—peel them, and throw them in the bucket. Now and again, two people lift the bucket and empty it into a tub filled with water.

"Your turn, Ahmet."

I rise.

Si-Ya-U turns to the girl with blue eyes: "You, too, Anushka."

She stands up: so she's tall. We grab the bucket, she at one end and I at the other. I can't get a sense of the shape of her legs: she's wearing felt boots. We empty the bucket into the tub. She washes her hands in the sink, white hands with long, plumpish fingers.

"Anushka, they'll get dirty again."

No response.

"Do you work in the office?"

"Why the familiar 'you'?"

Old Party members, especially Russian intellectuals, used the plural "you"; but young people at the university, whether we knew one another or not, used the singular.

"I see you're an old aristocrat."

"You don't look too proletarian yourself."

At lunch, I looked for Anushka in the dining hall, but I couldn't find her. This didn't stop me from devouring the cabbage soup, fat-free, and the black bread I had crumbled into it. And with the same gusto I drank the lukewarm tea that looked like dishwater.

The heavy, wet snow coming down since dawn in Moscow stopped in the afternoon and resumed at nightfall, but now it was fine, dry snow. Today was one chore after another. I climbed on top of crates of dried fish on the truck parked in the university courtyard. The truck had arrived late, and we couldn't unload it. My feet are freezing inside my army boots. I should get down and stomp on the snow. Which I did. I got down, stomped around, and warmed up. I could see the tower of the Strastnoi Monastery from the courtyard. A sledge drove by, the driver's strange turban covered with snow. The riders must be Nepmen; you can tell from their furs and kalpaks. I suppose you can't sing a song while on duty. Yet I feel like singing the Budyonni march at the top of my voice: *Dayosh Warsaw! Dayosh Berlin!* Give us Warsaw! Give us Berlin! It must be the gun I'm clutching so tight, or maybe the Nepmen I saw along Strastnoi Boulevard as it runs on and on in the dark under snow. I heard something move. An impossible idea flashed through my mind: maybe Anushka. I turned around. Under the lamplight, right next to me, stood a *bezprizorni*—one of those homeless, roaming street kids. Rags from head to toe. In what little was visible of his incredibly dirty face, his eyes shone bright. His little nose was red. He was about twelve.

"Hello, mister."

"Hello."

"It smells like fish, mister."

"Could be."

"Is the truck carrying fish?"

"It's carrying fish."

"Have you been on watch a long time, mister?"

"Long time."

"It smells like fish."

"Could be . . ."

"Can't you give me a fish, mister?"

"Can't be. Didn't you hit anything today?"

"Just a little bag. Empty."

"They house you guys some place. Feed and clothe you. Why don't you go?"

"I care about my freedom, mister."

"Where're you from?"

"Volga Valley."

"How'd you get here?"

"Walked. And a train. The sleeper."

"The crate between the wheels . . ."

"I guess. If you gave me one fish, one little tiny fish, would it be the end of the world?"

"I can't."

"Are the fish counted? One more, one less, who'd know?"

"I'd know."

"I swear I'm hungry."

"How about money?"

"Okay."

I gave him some. He stashed it in his rags somewhere.

"And give me a fish, too."

"I just gave you money."

"At this hour, all the shops are closed. You think money is good all the time? I'm hungry. A tiny fish?"

"Can't be."

"Why not, uncle?"

"If I gave everyone a fish, there'd be no fish left on the truck."

"Am I everyone?"

"Aren't you?"

"I'm not. I'm Six-fingered Fedya."

"Why 'six-fingered'?"

He pulled out his right hand; a piece of flesh dangled near his pinkie.

"Got a cigarette, mister?"

I gave him a cigarette.

"You want a light, too?"

"It's not good to smoke on an empty stomach. Give me a fish, too."

I gave a fish to Six-fingered Fedya from the Volga Valley.

"Can you give me one more?"

"No. You're going too far."

"Don't get mad. Take this back and give me a bigger one."

I took it back and gave him a bigger one. He stashed it in his rags somewhere.

"Why aren't you eating? Weren't you hungry?"

"I'll eat it with Sanka."

"And who's that?"

"My sweetheart."

"How old is she?"

"Younger than me. And a fish for her."

"Go on, beat it . . ."

"Don't get mad; I'm out of here."

He crossed his arms, hunched up his shoulders, and walked away. Then he stopped and looked back: "I won't tell anyone they're giving away fish here. If all the watchmen were like you, the Soviet government would be in one fine mess. Goodbye, uncle . . ."

He left the courtyard and vanished in the snowy darkness of Strastnoi Boulevard.

When I got back to the dorm, everyone was asleep. Only Si-Ya-U's bed, next to mine, was empty. As I unwound the rags I'd wrapped around my feet for socks, Si-Ya-U came in. He was the only student at the university with a frock coat. He even wore patent-leather shoes and a bow tie. He had a felt hat, too, but no longer used it. He went out wearing his felt hat once, and the kids on Tsvetnoy Boulevard started chasing him, shouting "Bourjouy!" His French was excellent. I think he came to Moscow from Paris, but I'm not really sure. Those who are not here with official passports—me among them—don't ask one another certain questions.

"Si-Ya-U, I've been meaning to ask. Who, exactly, is this Anushka?"

"The Director's secretary."

"I got that. I mean, who's her mother, her father?"

"Her father was an engineer. He was gunned down by the Kolchaks. Her mother died of typhus. *Bonne nuit.*"

The sound of the motor beats into the night. Ahmet dragged his bare feet to the bed. He lay on his back. Goodbye, Anushka!

．．．

When I woke up, strands of daylight penetrated the dark cottage through the cracks in the door. Ismail had closed the door when he left; I opened it. I drank tea from a very fine tea glass—no doubt left over from Ziya.

Ahmet turned on the lamp and closed the door. He could still hear the motor. I wonder if my pickax can be heard outside? He put the gun on the bed. And I should really secure this door. What good is that? If they raid me while I'm digging, a crossbar won't keep them out. He checked his watch: quarter-past eight. He started digging at the center of the cottage. He looked at his watch: nine-thirty. I'm out of breath after an hour and a quarter. Damn it. He drank some water. Lit a cigarette. Opened the door. The road below still wound its lonesome, dusty way in glaring sunlight.

Ahmet closed the door. He started shoveling the earth he had dug up into a corner. He looked at his watch: ten to twelve. My hands are blistered. The cottage is hot as a steam bath.

Moscow's cold is dry; it doesn't lash you with wind. Even Africans have no trouble taking it. I went to the Eastern Students' party in my combat boots, leggings, and Russian shirt of coarse cloth. Not that I could have worn anything else, even if I wanted to. They're dancing in the great hall. And it's packed. I saw Si-Ya-U. In his well-tailored navy-blue costume, he looked like he had changed clothes to attend a masked ball. He didn't see me.

I started sweating. Damn it. Ahmet wiped the sweat off his face with his bare arm. He had taken off his shirt. Leaning on his pickax, he straightened up.

Ah, Si-Ya-U is dancing—with Anushka! The girl saw me. She smiled. Her hair's straw-blond, her neck long and round. I looked at her legs: thick. Good—I'm happy I found a part of her that isn't beautiful.

. . .

Ahmet stepped outside, his jacket over his shoulder. I'm drenched in sweat; I could catch a cold in a minute, damn it. He devoured his noon ration—pastrami, bread, tomatoes. A bus passed by on the road below, kicking up clouds of dust. Ahmet closed the door. He thought he'd rest a minute, and lay face down on the bed. When he opened his eyes, Ismail stood over him: "Dead-tired, huh?"

"How many hours did I sleep?"

The cottage door stood open. A clear night had settled down outside.

Ahmet opened his suitcase.

Ismail asked: "Is the plan ready?"

"I started without a plan. But I'll draw one up. I saw a model in Moscow—at the Museum of the Revolution."

"I'll move out the dirt—after it gets dark. There's a big basket out back. Left over from Ziya. What was I going to say . . . The meeting is tomorrow night."

They sat on the threshold. Ismail had brought tahini helvah.

"Get me one Istanbul paper and one Izmir every day."

Ahmet holding one side of the pannier, Ismail the other, they carried out the dirt—the way I carried the potatoes with Anushka—up the hill.

"Tomorrow, Ismail, we'll leave the meeting separately. It's best no one knows I'm staying with you."

The following night, they came back late from the meeting, but they didn't go to bed before they hauled out the dirt Ahmet had dug up.

A rainy night—the first time I realized how different Izmir's summer showers are from Istanbul's. Handing over the day's papers to Ahmet, Ismail said: "The police are looking for you. They've been looking a week. They questioned two Ahmet Kadris from Istanbul."

"Şükrü Bey's work."

"Maybe. But he would have given a description of you. They wouldn't grab every Ahmet Kadri they found."

"I'm sure the guys they caught look like me. They'd have gotten my description from Istanbul. The question is, how did they find out I came to Izmir? And why this frantic search for me?"

"The arrests have begun."

"What're you saying?"

My heart is pounding—like the night I thought I was being followed. The newspapers wrote that Communists were arrested in Istanbul and Ankara and would be tried by the Independence Tribunal; they launched an intensive search for those they didn't catch. I'm one of those they didn't catch.

"Who all knew you were coming here?"

"Those who knew haven't been caught. Here, the police . . ."

"Wouldn't know them. Maybe they'll question Hüsnü, if they shut down the Railway Workers Association."

"They'll shut it down."

The rain stopped. The sound of the motor was muffled, diffused by the hot, humid night air.

They sat on the threshold and ate bread, olives, and tahini helvah.

"What do you think their sentence will be, Ahmet?"

"With the Independence Tribunal, you can never tell."

"Well, they won't hang them, brother!"

That day, full dark wasn't safe enough to carry out the dug-up dirt; they waited till it got very late. The opening of the hole was about a square meter; they decided they'd cover it up in two days. They'd make a wood crate, fill it level with earth, and drop it in the opening of the hole. The earth in the crate would blend with the earth floor, and the hole could be opened or closed whenever they wanted.

Ahmet no longer opens the door in daylight to sit on the threshold. All day, under the gas lamp, he reads the books left over from Ziya. One of them is a book of poems.

"Ismail, anything you remember from the poems here?"

"Just one line: 'The ship with a hundred masts, where is the port it sails for?'"

"Why do you remember that line?"

"Because of the masts."

The Izmir Railway Workers Association was shut down. Its managers and Hüsnü were questioned but let go.

A month passed. I didn't leave the cottage—not even once— the whole month. We postponed the meetings for a while. I finished the books left over from Ziya. I read the papers, down to the ads. I tried to draw a picture of the ship with a hundred masts, but couldn't.

Ismail slowly spread out on the table the provisions he had brought. He turned to Ahmet: "They put out a paper in Bursa—*Comrade*."

"How? When?"

"Before the arrests. I just learned today."

"And then?"

"It was banned."

When Ahmet left for Izmir, they told him in Istanbul: "Prepare the place for the secret press, but only the space. We'll let you know the next step." Ahmet now understands why they said this. They would go as far as they could legally to publish *Comrade*. Fine, but couldn't the paper for the press, the type, the ink, the pedals, all that shit and trash, be stored legally? So here we are with an empty hole. Did we think they'd follow the Constitution? Does our bourgeoisie give a damn about the Constitution? When the Kurdish rebellion broke out, we were the only ones who didn't call it a simple uprising of bandits. We said the lands of the Kurdish beys and sheiks must be handed over to the Kurdish peasants right away. We said that if the British and the Caliphate had their fingers in this pie, this was the only way to cut them off at the root. There shouldn't be bad blood between Turks and Kurds. On and on we wrote and wrote. And what happened?

Ismail spoke as if reading Ahmet's mind: "Brother, the bastards are determined to wipe us out at the roots."

"What did you think? Our aghas lost their revolutionary spirit long ago—at least eighty percent of them. We have to accept this fact, damn it."

Ten years later, in 1935, Ziya could give Ismail living proof of Ahmet's point. "Ismail," Ziya could have said, "do you know who I ran into yesterday? One of our senators who served as a judge on the Ankara Independence Tribunal in 1925. I asked the bastard: 'What was the account you couldn't settle with us ten years ago?'"

He gave me a knowing look.

"Dear Ziya Bey," he said, "you brought trouble upon yourselves. I have two farms. If we gave the Kurdish beys' lands to the Kurdish peasants, our peasants would want our lands. It would set a precedent, Ziya Bey, a precedent . . ."

Pushing on the table, Ahmet stood up. "I'm going to Istanbul, Ismail."

"Brother, are you crazy?"

"I have to tend to the paper, the pedal, all that stuff. And connect with friends."

"I'm sure nobody's left in Istanbul. And do you know how tight security is on trains and boats?"

They met at Hüsnü's house again. They decided Ahmet should not go. Another man (because Ahmet didn't quite trust him) was not sent to the Istanbul address.

I don't light the gas lamp during the day. I see the sunlight coming through the cracks in the door and watch the play, the dalliance, the merrymaking, the crazy revelry of the dust motes, and ask Anushka, "The ship with a hundred masts, where is the port it sails for?" Nights, I sat Ismail down and made two portraits of him. He liked one of them, the one that didn't look like him . . .

Three weeks passed.

To open the door and go out, to lie on my back on the hilltop where we spread the dug-up earth, for just ten minutes! I started calculating the time of Ismail's return, first by the hour and then by twenty-minute, then ten-minute intervals. In the end, I lost count. Prisoners are isolated in solitary for years. Yes, but they know beforehand they can't open their doors and step out. But if I wanted to, I could open the door right now and step outside. I am living the agony of not opening the door that I well know I can open.

Another week passed.

For maybe an hour, Ahmet has been peering outside, his eyes fixed on a door crack. And my heart beats *da-dum-da-dum*. I know I'm going to do something bad. I know I'm going to open that door. I'm being an ass. I know. Slowly I opened the door. Coming down the other slope of the hill, I could barely keep from running. I'd shaved my mustache. And put on Ismail's old overalls. And I'd blackened my face a little. I thought I looked like a blacksmith or something. I walked down the road about fifteen minutes. I stepped aside to make way for the bus headed to the city. I came to a fairly high wall, with a stone foundation, on my right. Above the wall, two people sat under a plane tree. And strings of tobacco leaves were hung to dry under a wooden roof raised on posts. A fountain stood below the wall. Stepping on the edge of the basin, I put my mouth to the faucet. Water soaked my chest and right arm, and feeling my upper lip utterly naked without the mustache—not that a *lower* lip could have a mustache—I drank and drank my fill. I straightened up. As I wiped my mouth with the back of my right hand, it felt like an iron bar hit the back of my left leg. I spun around: a yellow dog, grinning, baring his teeth—maybe not grinning, but afterwards I thought he was. He was drooling all over—maybe not, but afterwards I thought he was. The yellow dog quietly walked away, with his tail between his legs; I mean, without growling, as if scared off when our eyes met. I checked my leg. I looked at my hand: blood. The men above the wall had seen what happened. They called out, "Don't mind him, kid, just put some tobacco on it. What got into him? He's harmless." I took some tobacco from the box they tossed me, pressed it into the wound, and tied my handkerchief tight around it.

That night, it took Ismail a while to notice Ahmet had shaved his mustache. Ahmet was trying to trim the wick of the lamp with his nail clippers, and the sooty glitter of light flickered across his distracted face.

"Why'd you shave your mustache, brother?"

"Do I look different?"

"I didn't notice at first, but if I look for it, you've changed. You don't look right without a mustache."

"My nose is twice as long, right?"

That day, Ahmet kept what had happened a secret from Ismail. Both the shit I did and my hiding it from Ismail—it's shameful. But I covered it up.

Another four days passed.

Ahmet, dipping his huge tomato in salt, chomped on it while he read the Izmir paper. Ismail was changing the newspapers lining the food cupboard.

"Ismail!"

"What?"

"Look, the paper says rabid dogs are roaming around."

"They're around. They bit a couple kids. And the day before yesterday, the guard at the factory."

"So what'll happen now, Ismail?"

"What'll happen? They send those bitten to Istanbul. That's the only rabies hospital"

"Has anyone gotten rabies?"

"Sure."

"And the owners of the rabid dogs, what penalty . . ."

"Brother, who's going to own up to a rabid dog?"

"Goddamn it. Ismail, let's have a meeting tomorrow."

I told him what had happened.

"That's the way it is, Ismail . . ."

Ismail repeated, "That's the way it is." Then: "The dog belongs to the tobacco growers you saw above the wall. Ziya and I had coffee many times under that plane tree. I'll go see tomorrow. The dog will be there. If he were rabid, he'd have bitten someone else before you. And the tobacco men would have killed him long ago."

"Why couldn't I be the one he might have bitten before me? Why couldn't he have started with me?"

"He may have. It could be. But, brother, why think the worst that can happen?"

The meeting again took place at Hüsnü's house: a stone-paved yard, an unpainted wooden house, two upstairs rooms, the windows covered with lattice screens. Once again, people take off their shoes at the door, under the nightlight, and walk up to the second floor and enter the room on the left. I love the spotless divans with their cambric covers. The floorboards, bleached white from much washing and scrubbing, are still damp. Again, it smells of white soap, lavender—Edirne soap, I think—and damp pine boards. In the next room, Hüsnü's six-month-old daughter is crying. Hüsnü called the meeting to order. I told my story. Ismail spoke: "I went to see the tobacco growers. They said the dog was run over by a bus."

Hüsnü, his beard still overgrown, his flannel shirt spotless as always, asked: "When?"

"This morning."

"How do we know he was run over? Maybe the guys are afraid they'd have to pay a fine—afraid of getting into trouble. Maybe they're lying."

"Are you trying to say the dog was rabid?"

Hüsnü, avoiding Ahmet's eyes across from him, turned to Ismail: "Could be. When you talked with these guys, did you tell them their dog bit Ahmet?"

"Are you crazy?"

The young woman, her head covered with a white scarf, served coffee again. Every time she bent down, her milk-heavy breasts filled out the neckline of her loose dress again. And one felt the utmost respect for this woman.

Slurping his coffee, Ahmet tried to talk as if he had nothing to do with the topic: "So the dog died of rabies, and the owners say he was run over by a bus, because they're afraid of having to pay a fine? Maybe. As Hüsnü says, 'Could be.' But maybe the dog wasn't rabid, and he really was run over by a bus. He bit me because he's a dog, not because he is rabid; this could also be. Right, Ismail?"

"Could be. Wait, I just remembered—he once tried to bite Ziya's hand."

Hüsnü asked: "Why?"

"Ziya was holding out a bone and taking it back, teasing the dog."

Ahmet patiently listened to the conversation, then said: "I didn't take the dog's bone. But he could have bit me just because he's a dog. If so, you can censure me for a lack of discipline, for going outside, and the subject is closed." I took a deep breath; partly in pain, my heart beat faster and faster. What if the dog was rabid and died? So he was rabid when he bit me. So I'm going to be rabid. Suddenly I wanted to laugh—there was something comical about the word *rabid*. Damn it. I have to go to Istanbul and get rabies shots, so I don't get rabid . . . The head doctor of the rabies hospital knows me.

Hüsnü spoke: "We decided against your going to Istanbul. But these events change the situation. Maybe you can make it to Istanbul without getting caught by the police, and if the doctor knows you, maybe he won't tell them . . ."

The woman in the white scarf came in, gathered up the cups, and left. I spoke: "Let's sum up the situation." Everyone has long grasped the situation, but I'm making it very clear again. Out of pigheadedness. "There are three possible scenarios. First, the dog is rabid. Either I'm caught on my way to Istanbul, or the doctor informs the police. He won't risk vaccinating a wanted man without reporting him. I don't turn rabid—they still give me the shots, but I'm in the hands of the Independence Tribunal. This is the first scenario. As for the second, the dog is rabid. I don't get caught on the way to Istanbul. And the doctor turns out to have courage. I get the shots, I don't get rabies. I'm safe. Now the third scenario: the dog is not rabid. I'm caught on my way to Istanbul, or the doctor calls the police. I'm in the hands of the Independence Tribunal for nothing. I surrender, like a fool. Ah, there's yet another scenario: the dog is rabid. I don't go to Istanbul to get shots. I get rabid here. Should I go or not?"

They reached no decision. "Do what you want," they said.

Again, Ahmet left early. Ismail again caught up with him where they could hear the motor. They walked in silence.

As he lit the lamp and started undressing, Ahmet said, "I'm not going to Istanbul."

Ismail was quiet. He got in bed. Ahmet reached over to his pants on the chair. I took out the gun in my back pocket and laid it on Ismail's clothes on the other chair.

"I'm turning the gun over to you, Ismail."

"Why?"

"There's a fifty-percent chance I'll get rabies."

"If you tried to go to Istanbul?"

"No. The chance the dog is rabid is fifty percent. The chance the doctor will inform the police is one-hundred percent. Plus, the possibility of getting caught on the way. I'm not going to Istanbul. If I get rabid, shoot me. Dump me in this hole and cover me up with dirt. So I don't smell."

I say these things—"shoot me," "dump me," "in this hole," and especially "so I don't smell"—as if to spite Ismail.

"Nobody knows I'm here anyway." I smile. "But just in case, I'll write a note. I'll say I took my life for a hopeless passion." This is the lowest I have ever sunk. Damn it. "Well, that's the way it is, Ismail."

"I swear you're crazy."

"Crazy what? What? When I jump on you and try to bite? Huh?"

Ismail didn't answer.

"Do you know how to use a gun, Ismail?"

"I know."

"Are you a good shot?"

"Pretty good."

I paced up and down. I stopped at the food cupboard. I opened and closed its door.

"Now go to bed, brother."

"Find me a medical book tomorrow."

"For what?"

"I'll read up on rabies symptoms. As far as I know, you don't get rabid in one day. We'll see if this shit has phases and crises. Before you turn rabid and attack, drooling and howling . . ."

"Where do you get the howling, brother?"

"I saw a play in Istanbul once. Muhsin put it on. 'The Lighthouse Watchmen' or something like that. In a lighthouse out at sea, on a night when all ties to land were cut, a truly stormy night, one of the watchmen—the son, I think—goes rabid and attacks the other watchman, his father. In that play, he howls."

"Go to bed. And turn off the light."

"Don't forget the book."

"I won't—if I can find one."

"What do you mean if you can find one? Find one and bring it."

"Okay, okay."

Tonight the motor pounded inside the cottage.

"Ismail . . ."

"What?"

"Are you sleeping?"

"Can't."

Moonlight streamed into the dark cabin through the cracks in the door.

"What're you thinking, Ismail?"

"Nothing . . ."

But he was thinking. Ahmet now wanted the whole world, and especially Ismail, to think only about him. And it's understandable. But Ismail's mind was on his own mother.

THE SIXTH LINE

AHMET FLIPPED THE BOOK Ismail had handed him over on the bed. They ate in silence. They lit their cigarettes, and Ahmet asked: "Did you look it up in the book, Ismail?"

"I did."

"So, does a man howl like a dog?"

"He does."

"What else does it say?"

"Read, you'll see."

"The fortieth day. . . ."

"Yes, forty, forty-one days, it says."

Ahmet didn't open the book. He placed it on his clothes and blew out the lamp. They were quiet for a while. Ismail: "Who're you fooling, brother? Turn on the light and read it."

I turned on the lamp. I read: nothing more than what I'd picked up here and there. First, headaches, joint pains, fatigue, and so on, then loss of appetite, fear for no reason, then fear of water, of fire, then drooling and the ordeal of wanting to attack and bite, and then howling. Paralysis comes on the fortieth or forty-first day.

I got up. I took a chalk stick out of my charcoal box. On the door I drew six lines. Six white lines.

"What's that, Ahmet?"

"Today is the sixth day, Ismail."

"By God, brother, you're crazy."

Ismail lit a cigarette and handed one to Ahmet. He doesn't like what he sees: the kid won't get rabies, but he'll torture himself for forty days.

Ismail blew out the lamp. In the dark, Ahmet can see the six white lines on the door.

• • •

On the seventh day, Anushka saw the lines I'd drawn on the door of the dacha.

"What are these, Ahmet?"

"It's our seventh day. So we have thirteen days left, Anushka."

"Then what?"

"Then, you know, your leave is over, my vacation ends, and we go back to Moscow . . ."

"Say, Ahmet . . ."

"What?"

"Last night you screamed in your sleep, as if you were strangling. You must have had a weight on your chest."

"Well, it's not because I'm rabid. Even the headaches haven't started yet. I do this a couple times a year. Next time, just nudge me lightly, that's enough. I want to wake up, but I can't. Damn it. Most of the time I know where I am, but sometimes I think I'm in a totally different place. I feel I'll die if I don't wake up that instant. Once, Anushka . . . As I said, don't be afraid, just nudge me lightly, that's enough."

Ismail hadn't taken the gun when he left this morning.

"Take the gun tomorrow, Ismail."

Ismail didn't answer. He was asleep.

Batum is a chessboard of a city. It can rain for forty days and nights in Batum, but when the sun comes out, the pebble-paved streets dry off in a flash.

I sat at the table in the Hôtel de France in Batum. All varieties of tropical trees, flowers, grasses—they're all in Batum in the Greenpoint Botanical Gardens to look at, touch, and smell. In 1922, midsummer, men and women lay side by side on the Batum beach, face down or on their backs—all completely naked. I mean, no bathing suits or anything, just stark naked. I'd landed here from Anatolia, having seen only the hands and feet of women exposed, plus their eyes, and that only from glimpsing them in market places. But sometimes, in a marketplace, meeting a pair of eyes between two pieces of cloth, I have felt as if I'd seen the woman naked from head to toe, or even worse . . . As with all absolute things, one quickly gets used to absolute nakedness, when nothing is left to the imagination. Before long, I barely noticed the nakedness of the women lying on the beach in Batum.

In Batum, in the Hôtel de France, I sat down at the table in my room. The Red Cavalry passes down below on the street. They're tired, half-hungry, but the world is all theirs. Tonight there's a meeting, and I'm going. The nonstop clatter of wooden soles of shoes and sandals on the pebble streets of Batum. Clickety-clack, clickety-clack, click . . .

In the Hôtel de France, I sat down at the table. And I'm really, really starved. Along with a quarter loaf of bread a day, I have two meals of corn soup and drink two glasses of tea with saccharin. Fish heads swim in it—in the soup, not the tea. I sold my patent-leather shoes long ago. A young peasant from Adjara bought them. He was getting married. He bought my shoes as a present for his bride. For how many million rubles! I asked the crew and the officers on the Turkish boat that took me from Trabzon to Batum: "Is money still good in Batum? If it's Communist, as far as I know money must have been abolished." "Money's still good with the Mensheviks but not the Bolsheviks," they said; "We don't know about communism, but since the Bolsheviks control Batum . . ." I had fifty liras. I handed it out to the crew. I saved only one lira as a historical curiosity. The boat that carried me to Batum took on guns and ammunition and returned to Trabzon. I later learned that some of the crew and some of the officers—they must have been the ones who said they didn't know about communism—were also involved in smuggling jewelry at the time.

I sat down at the table in the Hôtel de France in Batum. A table with carved legs—not just the legs but the whole gilded oval table was covered with intricate carvings. Rococo . . . In the seaside house in Üsküdar, a rococo table sits in the guestroom. Ro-co-co ... The journey I made from the Black Sea coast to Ankara, then from there to Bolu, the thirty-five-day, thirty-five-year journey on foot to the town where I taught school— in short, to make a long story short, the encounter of a pasha's descendant—more precisely, a grandson—with Anatolia now rests on the rococo table in the Hôtel de France in Batum, spread out over the table like a tattered, dirty, blood-stained block-print cloth. I look, and I want to cry. I look, and my blood rushes to my head in rage. I look, and I'm ashamed again. Of the house by the sea in Üsküdar. *Decide, son,* I say to myself, *decide.* The decision was made: death before turning back. Wait, don't rush, son. Let's put the questions on this table, right next to Anatolia here. What can you sacrifice for this cause? What can you give? Everything. Everything I have. Your freedom? Yes! How many years can you rot in prison for this cause? All my life, if necessary! Yes, but you like women, fine dining, nice clothes. You can't wait to travel, to see Europe, Asia, America, Africa. If you just leave Anatolia here on this rococo table in Batum and go from Tbilisi to Kars and back to Ankara from there, in five or six years you'll be a senator, a minister—women, wining and dining, art, the whole world. No! If necessary, I can spend my whole life in prison. Okay, but what about getting hanged, killed, or drowned like Mustafa Suphi and his friends if I become a Communist—didn't you ask yourself these questions in Batum? I did. I asked myself, Are you afraid of being killed? I'm not afraid, I said. Just like that, without thinking? No. I first knew I was afraid, then I knew I wasn't. Okay, are you ready to be disabled, crippled, or made deaf for this cause? I asked. And TB, heart disease, blindness? Blindness? Blindness ... Wait a minute—I hadn't thought about going blind for this cause. I got up. I shut my eyes tight and walked around the room. Feeling the furniture with my hands, I walked around the room in the darkness of my closed eyes. Twice I stumbled, but I didn't open my eyes. Then I stopped at the table. I opened my eyes. Yes, I can accept blindness. Maybe I was a bit childish, a little comical. But this is the truth. Not books or word-of-mouth propaganda or my social condition brought me where I am. Anatolia brought me where I am. The Anatolia I had seen only on the surface, from the outside. My heart brought me where I am. That's how it is . . .

THE SEVENTH LINE

WHEN ISMAIL got out of bed at the crack of dawn, Ahmet had been long awake. But he pretended to be asleep. He watched Ismail through slit eyes. Ismail got dressed. He picked up the gun, turned it around, looked it over, and stuck it in his pocket. He took sausage and bread from the food cupboard and ate standing up. He quietly opened the door and quietly pulled it shut behind him. Ahmet watched it all through slit eyes. Suddenly he felt something missing from the cottage or outside it: the road, the wall under the plane tree, Hüsnü's divans, Şükrü Bey's courtyard, the burnt-out fields, the city of Izmir, Tverskoy Boulevard in Moscow, Anushka's dacha, the sea, the world. Something had vanished. When? While he was asleep? But he'd been awake for three hours. But he just suddenly realized, right then, that something was gone. Maybe suddenly, just this instant, the sound of the motor stopped, just suddenly shut off. Ahmet pricked up his ears, not for patters or murmurs but for silence.

Si-Ya-U, as usual, tiptoed into the room. He had never come back this late, at dawn. It's snowing outside the frosted storm windows. I know where Si-Ya-U has been. He sat on the table.

The table must be over two meters long and eighty or ninety centimeters wide. Why not a meter? I'll have to measure it. Is it longer than the hole? Damn it, did I dig my own grave? There's a song—"Dig my grave on the roadside." My nanny used to sing it in the house by the sea, and I used to cry. Ismail took the gun.

Si-Ya-U got up from the table. He took from his nightstand his carving set and the piece of ivory. He's chiseling and filing the ivory. He has his hat on. They gave us this room two months ago, because I was the head of the Turkish students' fine arts club and he the head of the Chinese. Si-Ya-U used to show me his ivory carvings as he worked on them: Chinese girls, one more delicate and more beautiful than the other, all melancholy, all looking alike—slender, curving and undulating upward like vines, up to twenty centimeters—and bald, beardless old Chinese men sitting cross-legged, resting their oiled naked bellies on their knees. But he's worried I'll see the piece of ivory he's been working on for the last month. And I pretend not to see. But I know whose face he's carving in ivory . . . The alarm clock went off. Si-Ya-U put his stuff into his pockets. When did he take off his hat? I must have dozed off at some point. The alarm clock rings nonstop.

I never once heard Ismail's alarm clock. It's always under his pillow.

"Did you just get back, Si-Ya-U?"

"Why?"

"Your bed's still made."

He doesn't say anything. He's clearly upset that I don't understand he doesn't want to tell me when he came in or, worse, that I know and still ask him.

"Were you with Anushka again?"

He looks at me as if I've done something shameful. I say, "I know you love the girl."

He says nothing. He's still looking at me just like that.

"Why would you keep such a thing secret from a friend? Does Anushka love you, too?" I'm ashamed of myself, but his being with Anushka till early morning—I don't think of them kissing or anything, I know they just walk by the Moscow River, not even holding hands, I saw them myself—but his being with Anushka till the small hours drives me crazy, and I've just realized it drives me crazy.

"Anushka loves you, too, right?"

"No."

It has stopped snowing. A few people sit on the benches on Tverskoy Boulevard. I walk up to Strastnoi Square. Sledges drive past. This dog is a German shepherd, not gold but dark. German shepherds are not golden. He walks alongside a little girl.

A rabid dog is low and sneaky. He creeps up behind you, quietly, and sinks his teeth into the back of your left leg. Ismail didn't close the door tight when he left; I can see the early light through the opening.

I'm working on a piece on the effects of the Great October Revolution on Russian and world art. I'm in the university library. The silence reminds me of the stillness of the backyard, in the fall, of the seaside house in Üsküdar. Before me lie books and documents on my topic. I haven't touched them tonight. I don't feel like working. I had no appetite today for even my favorite class, Political Economy. Only two people in the library besides me. One is Russian. Young. He lost both arms in the civil war. He turns the leaves of his book with a wood stick between his teeth. I don't know the other one, but his clothes and facial features say he's Mongolian. The issues of *Pravda* on the empty table on the left caught my eye. I picked up a volume. 1922. On the first page, headlines and New Year's messages: "Remember, comrades! If the workers and peasants don't extend their generosity, the New Year means new graveyards in the Volga Valley! Our New Year's wishes: the defeat of hunger, revived industries, an abundant harvest, and the triumph of the proletarian revolution around the world!" I look at other news: war of national liberation in Egypt. The Czechoslovak government sends three million krones for the hungry in Russia. I turn the pages. 3 January: general strike of railway workers in Germany. Printers strike in China. Miners in England prepare to strike. 10 January: Baku's oil production rises. Street fighting in Ireland. Headlines on 14 January: "When you get your paycheck, remember the hungry! As you feed your children, don't forget the orphans who lost their mothers and fathers to hunger in the Volga Valley!" I'm searching for news of Turkey. I find it—7 February, Comrade Frunze's statement upon his return from Ankara: Ukraine and Turkey have reached an agreement. The National Assembly favors friendly relations with Russia. 10 February, Comrade Frunze again: "In the past, in the Tsarist era, fear of imperialism descending from the north, a fear of Moscow, poisoned the majority of the Turkish people. This fear had been engrained in the Turkish soul. Now, on the contrary, the Turkish people harbor great friendship for Russia, Ukraine, and the other Soviet republics." I found another piece of news in March: we have thanked the Soviet government for requesting Turkey be invited to the Geneva Conference.

Petrosian came in, the secretary of the university's Party cell. He's not wearing his Red Flag Medal today. He looked over my shoulder at the pages of *Pravda* spread out before me. I whispered: "The papers of '22. It feels like ten years have gone by, not a year."

Petrosian nodded, whispering: "There's an article about the problems with our agricultural policies. If you run across it, jot down the date somewhere—it's either December or November."

"Will do."

Petrosian left. He's working on a study of land questions in the Middle East. "If I work real hard, it'll be done in three years," he says. But he has cancer. Even he knows he won't live more than eight or nine months, a year at most.

Iran has donated three hundred *puts* of rice and twenty-three *puts* of raisins for the starving children in the Volga Valley. The United States has shipped seven freighters of corn. The British cabinet refused monetary aid to Russia. I'm at 15 March. Again the headlines: "Every organization, every citizen must answer, with their hands on their consciences, whether they have done everything they could to aid the famine victims. Those who have plugged their ears to shut out the wails of people starving to death should be nailed to a cross. And branded as murderers!" Swedish Communists have sent 1560 *puts* of flour and fish and twenty thousand krones. Lenin speaks at the eleventh assembly of the Russian Communist Party. Fascist dictatorship in Italy. More news from us: Turkish Communists extended their congratulations to the Red Army on the liberation of Vladivostok. The National Assembly voted to terminate the Istanbul government.

Outside the window, snowflakes—big, wet, soft—settled on the Moscow night. The young amputee rapidly turned the pages of the book before him with the little wood stick between his teeth.

Headlines, 7 November: "We salute you, Western workers who support the Russian Workers' Republic. We salute the ironworkers of Germany, you who brought down Kaiser Wilhelm. Now take down the bloody throne of Stiness!" In the same issue, Lenin's tribute: "Esteemed comrades! I congratulate you all on the fifth anniversary of the October Revolution. This is my wish: in the coming five years, let us achieve no less in peace than we have achieved with arms. Yours, Lenin." In the same issue: "Youth, make haste—come take the place of generations past!"

Hasan walked in. He pretended not to see me. He sat at a table on my left. Hasan had been a junior officer in the Ottoman Army. He was taken prisoner while fighting the Tsarist armies in the Caucasus and sent to work in Siberia. He joined the Bolsheviks in '18. He met Mustafa Suphi in '19. There is hardly a front where he didn't fight the Whites—the Kolchaks, the Czechs, and Vrangel— and he also fought in the Turkish regiment Mustafa Suphi assembled against the Tashnaks and the Georgian Mensheviks. Now he's studying philosophy at the university, but he wants to be an electrical engineer. He doesn't like me, I think because I walked into the university in Moscow swinging my arms, without firing a single bullet at the enemies of the people, the capitalists, the imperialists. And he can't forgive me my pasha grandfather. (In 1932 Hasan became an electrical engineer. In 1937 he died before a firing squad; his name was cleared following the XXth Congress.) I went back to *Pravda*, 7 November 1922: "The comrades put in chains by the gendarmes of the bourgeoisie—the comrades serving prison sentences, those persecuted, exiled, tortured, or hanged for their committed service to socialism, we salute you on the fifth anniversary of the victory of the proletariat, in defiance of all prison walls and borders!"

Anushka walked in. I bent my head lower over *Pravda*, but I watched her out of the corner of my eye. She saw me. She wanted to walk up to me, then changed her mind. I think she sat at a table behind me, close to the door.

Pravda says, "We must purge Siberia of the Japanese." It says, "We must stand firm against international capital." "We must find a common business language with America," it says. "The budget must be balanced! We can't let our factories stand idle!" I found the article Petrosian was looking for: "The issues facing our agricultural policies." 21 December 1922. I got up. Just as I thought, Anushka sat behind me at a table close to the door.

"Come outside for a while."

I walked into the corridor; she followed.

"What do you want?"

"Did you walk along the Moscow River with Si-Ya-U last night?"

"What's it to you?"

"The guy is madly in love with you."

She didn't answer. Her blue eyes grew dark.

"And you love Si-Ya-U."

"Why wouldn't I love him? What do you want from me? Why did you call me outside?"

"What were you reading just now?"

She smiled. Her right cheek dimpled, but only her right. "Yesenin. Anything else you want to ask?"

"No."

"No, Ismail, that's not it. She wasn't playing hard to get. I thought of everything, but I never thought she was acting. If there was an ounce of acting, I would have picked it up. I would have picked up on it immediately. Plus, why would she be after me? Everyone at the university is chasing her. But she's close only to Si-Ya-U. She jokes and laughs and dances and hangs out with all the others, too, but that's all. Not that anyone thinks of going further. Well, maybe they do, but everyone holds back—if others saw what was on their minds, they'd be humiliated. I mean, thinking of going further would be like taking opium or something. We don't know what that'd be like, maybe we haven't even heard of any such thing. But if we knew and had taken opium and later sobered up, we'd be a laughing stock, no? That's how it was . . ."

That night, the Chinese were celebrating the anniversary of an important revolutionary event in their history. Si-Ya-U got Ahmet into the theater of the University Club shortly before the doors opened. Bunches of flowers framed the stage.

"Where did you find all these flowers in the dead of winter?"

They were paper flowers. Si-Ya-U laid an apricot rose leaf in Ahmet's palm; on the leaf was a red ladybug spotted white. From paper.

"Who'll see this ladybug, Si-Ya-U?"

"Anyone who cares. Plus, we wanted to prove our workmanship to ourselves."

Banners with Chinese characters streamed down the walls. I can write my name in Chinese script.

The students and their guests, all raucous, pushed and elbowed their way into the hall. The most striking were not the Chinese, the Japanese, or even the Africans but the Caucasians and the Central Asians. It must have been their clothing. In the city, too, they walked around in their local dress, sporting guns and daggers. The Central Asian young men were more handsome than the girls. On the stage, over the presidium, hung pictures of Marx, Engels, Lenin, and the Bolshevik Party leaders. Marx and Engels were placed highest up and framed in flowers. Applauding, we voted in about twenty comrades, leaders of the international Communist movement, as honorary members of the presidium. Petrosian turned the meeting over to Li, a mountain of a man. Those who don't know Chinese—that is, the majority—look at the Chinese for clues, and after a slight time lag they applaud, periodically interrupting Li's speech. I see the earth bound in chains. A worker at least three times the size of the globe brings his sledgehammer down on the chains. I hear the sound of the heavy, rusty chain links as they shatter and fly into the air.

On my left, in front of me, I saw Anushka sitting between an old Englishman working in the Comintern and an Indian student. They translated Li's speech into Russian. I believed everything Li said. I saw Capital, a huge spider with a pig's head, at the center of a web of smoke spun from factory chimneys. It plunged its stubby fingers, loaded with diamond rings, into a pile of gold coins. Anushka turned around; our eyes met. She smiled with the edges of her full lips. Anushka's ears look younger than her—about fourteen or so. On the stage, a Ukranian girl spoke in Ukranian. With her left hand, Anushka lifted the hair off her neck. I learned the name of the Ukranian girl: Lena. Last name: Yurchenko. Yurchenko had brown hair. When she talked, she had dimples on both cheeks. Not just on the right cheek, like Anushka. Something about her reminds me of Istanbul girls. I've never seen such good legs. I understand what the Ukranian girl says. A hand had scored *III International* on a wall. Below the wall, Capital shrank in horror, knocked down, his top hat thrown to one side, his fat belly to the other . . . We all stood and sang the "International," everyone in their own language, except everyone sang the word *international* together at the same time, the Chinese in Chinese.

In the lobby I asked Anushka: "Are you staying for the concert?"

"No. I'm leaving."

"Can I walk you home?"

It was a dark night. The snow couldn't light it up. It wasn't cold as we strolled down the boulevard toward the Moscow River.

Anushka said: "They killed my father before my eyes."

"The Kolchaks shot him, right?"

"They knocked on our door. My mother opened it. They walked into my father's room. I was there. Two officers. The first, the blond one with big blue eyes, pulled out his gun and shot my father in the head. Three times."

I didn't ask, "Then what did they do to you, and how did you get here from Siberia? Where did your mother die of typhus?" I said: "I paint pictures. I mean, I'm a painter."

"I know. I saw your room."

"When did you come to our room?"

"I liked one of the pictures a lot. A couple were so-so. But I didn't like most of them at all."

Why did Si-Ya-U keep Anushka's visit secret from me? When could she have come? What did they do? I felt my heart being ripped out. Then I was horribly ashamed by what flashed before my mind's eye. Anushka and Si-Ya-U—the bastard . . .

"Why aren't you talking?"

"Si-Ya-U is carving an ivory figure of you, isn't he?"

"I don't know. I asked him to carve a cat for me. I love cats. But he can't do it. He doesn't know how to make a cat."

"Bring your cat over; I'll paint him."

"But I don't have a cat."

"Then I'll paint from memory. A big Angora cat."

We entered the garden of Hram Spasitel Church facing the Moscow River. Anushka: "This is the first time I've been here at night in the winter."

The benches placed among the thick, snow-covered shrubbery were all taken. We sat on a bench further off, out in the open.

"Anushka, do you find me rude, impertinent?"

"No, but it might be better if you didn't, sometimes, overdo bad manners to make people forget your pasha grandfather."

"Did you hear about my grandfather from one of the Turks here? I can't think who'd have told you . . ."

"No one told me. I read it in your survey entry."

"Do you read the survey forms of all the students?"

"No. I read yours."

I didn't ask why. She would have given me a sensible answer. But I had already given myself the least sensible answer.

Suddenly, we heard whirring whistles everywhere—the militia. People scrammed, screaming.

"Two more here!"

Before Ahmet and Anushka knew what was happening, a militiaman with a bristly mustache yelled: "March!"

Ahmet saw a small crowd of men and women driven out of the garden. This was happening to him for the first time, but he had heard about it from friends. He understood what was going on. He told the militiaman who'd grabbed Anushka by the arm: "Take your hands off the girl! We're university students."

"I'm not a student, I'm a secretary at the university."

"Save it for the station!"

He blew his whistle several more times. Another militiaman appeared. No mustache.

"They're resisting."

Anushka freed her arm from the grasp of the bristly mustache: "We're not resisting. What's happening? What do you want from us? Why do we have to go to the station?"

"What were you doing here?"

"Just sitting."

"So you were just sitting, like brother and sister?"

"Yes, we were, "Ahmet said.

"Like brother and sister?"

Ahmet repeated the clean-shaven militiaman's words: "Like brother and sister."

"You don't look to me like anyone's brother. Are you Georgian?"

"I'm Turkish. A political emigrant. A Communist."

The clean-shaven militiaman ran his flashlight over the papers and the booklet Ahmet had handed him. He asked the bristly mustache: "Did you catch these two doing anything?"

"No-o-o . . . But what're they doing here? Anyway, they were *going* to do something . . ."

Anushka: "We didn't know this was a bad place."

"Now you know."

"We won't come here again."

"If you want, you can stay a while longer, but if I were you, I'd get out of here now."

Ahmet and Anushka walked out of the church garden. Without knowing it, they were both smiling. They didn't talk. They felt funny, a little shameful, and warm inside. Especially Ahmet. In the dark under the arch of the courtyard, he suddenly kissed Anushka. The girl did not resist. She gave herself to my mouth. A light from my heart illuminated me head to toe. Anushka didn't know how to kiss. I took her face in my hands: "Look me in the eye, girl. Haven't you kissed anyone before?"

"I have . . ."

"You're lying."

"Leave me alone."

I wanted to kiss her again. She pulled back.

In the afternoon, I sit drawing a cat. In three months this is my eighth or ninth cat. Spring rains come down on Moscow.

Si-Ya-U: "Anushka loves you."

"What gives you that idea?"

"She told me herself."

The motor goes *dum-dum-da-dum-dum*.

"Blow out the lamp, Ahmet."

Before blowing out the lamp, Ahmet gets up and draws the seventh line on the door. "Ismail, tell everyone I went to Istanbul. If anything happens, it's better they don't know I'm here."

"Yes, yes. Now go to bed."

The motor hums *dum-dum-da-dum-dum*.

The Fourteenth Line

AHMET DIDN'T WAIT till night. He drew the fourteenth line on the door a couple hours after Ismail left. He knew it was the fourteenth, but he counted anyway. Fourteen. Forty-one minus fourteen: twenty-seven left. He looked out through the cracks of the door. He pulled right back. Then he looked out again. A young woman in a yellow scarf and shalwars, barefoot and dark, was draping her wash over the bushes. By her side, a bare-chested boy. The boy looked toward the cottage. Ahmet stepped back, as if he could be seen behind the door. They must be Gypsies. He could hear them. The boy says, "I'm going in that cottage." The woman says, "You can't. Don't you see the padlock?" The boy says, "I can pick the lock." He starts tinkering with the lock. Ahmet retreats to the left corner. The boy peers through the cracks in the door. "A lamp's on in there!" the boy says. Inside, Ahmet curses the boy, the lamp, himself. The boy works at the lock, the woman hollers. Through the cracks, Ahmet sees the jostling shadows. The boy screams. She must be beating him. Then the woman and the boy disappear from the door cracks.

Ahmet stands in the corner, motionless, maybe ten minutes, maybe two hours; then he tiptoes to the door—am I crazy? How can they hear me from the outside? I'm barefoot. The woman squats by the clothes; the boy lies on his back. I retreated to my corner, reached for the chair, and sat down. And I crossed my hands on my belly. The woman starts singing. Her voice is warm. They say Gypsy women are hot. The lamp is just about out of gas. Damn it. Ahmet got up; on his way to the gas tank, he remembered there was no gas. Ismail would bring some tonight. He returned to his chair. The boy is talking with a man. He says a lamp's on in there. The man says, "The owner probably forgot to turn it off when he left this morning." They walked up to the door.

They looked in. The lamp sputtered and went out. "He turned off the lamp," the boy says. The woman yells, "What's somebody's lamp to you?" "Fairies are in there," the boy says.

Then all was quiet. Ahmet got up and looked out: nobody there, not even the clothes. He stuffed the door cracks with newspapers. He lay back on the bed. Pitch-black. Death is not even pitch-black. Not even headaches, dread, convulsions, drooling, and howling. And it's not Ismail shooting me with a gun. I feel the pain of something that's not even pitch-black. Death is not even pain. Damn it.

Ismail came in. "They've put up a tent on the left hillside," he said. "They'll probably be gone tomorrow. Ziya loved Gypsies; he'd say, 'If I hadn't sworn off marriage, I'd marry a Gypsy.'"

They ate inside the cottage. They didn't open the door. Ismail: "If they found a pill for rabies, if you didn't need shots . . . They will. You'll see. One day, they will."

Ahmet: "Before they find the pill, I'll have swallowed the pill." He smiled. He was embarrassed at the pun that had just slipped out.

"Nothing will happen," Ismail said. He glanced at the door— at the lines, no doubt.

"Fourteen lines," said Ahmet.

Toward midnight, Ahmet thought somebody was knocking on the door. He jumped awake on his cot.

I opened the door.

Ahmet rubbed his forehead. He's looking toward the door. Is this a raid or something? He listened. Only the motor: *dum-dum-da-dum-dum.*

I opened the door. It's 1921. We're in Inebolu—three days and four nights now. Two men I don't know stand at the door of our hotel room. I hear the rustle of the Black Sea. Two men in breeches and kalpaks stand at the door of our hotel room, lit from behind by the gas lamp far down the corridor.

Süleyman and Tevfik sat up on their beds. One of the men in breeches: "Get dressed, gentlemen."

Tevfik asked: "What's happening?"

"And take your bags, too."

Süleyman asked: "Me, too?"

"You, too."

We're in the half-dark of the night lamp. Tevfik asked: "And who are you?"

"From Ayin-Pe."

Ayin-Pe: Military Police.

The second man said to me: "Don't trouble yourself, bey."

The first man turned on the gas lamp in the room.

"Don't make a sound."

He's talking to Süleyman and Tevfik, not me.

Süleyman's hands shook as he packed his suitcase.

The first man walked them out ahead of him. The second man said to me: "Don't leave before we come for you tomorrow. We're returning your friends to Istanbul in an hour, on the next boat. Good night."

He left. I suddenly realized that Süleyman and Tevfik hadn't even said goodbye to me. It felt strange.

Four days before, my grandfather had left for the Üsküdar Pier Mosque for his morning prayers, and Süleyman, Tevfik, and I had left Istanbul for Inebolu.

There were two ways to get out of Occupied Istanbul to the Nationalists in Anatolia: by land via Pendik or by the Black Sea.

One of the people in charge of an organization smuggling arms from Istanbul to Mustafa Kemal was Süleyman's relative. He secured us three sets of forged travel papers. We got on the boat in Sirkeci, a bare-bones flat boat—it looked like those starching irons laundries use. We stepped into our cabin: it was cramped and hot as hell, with roaches crawling on the walls. Tevfik leaned his head against the porthole and wept. "So we won't see Istanbul again? Is this the point of no return?"

When the boat started shaking with the rumbling of the props, I stepped out on deck. Süleyman's relative had told us: "Stay in your cabin until you're in the clear, out on the Black Sea," but the rumbling of the props made me bold. And, anyway, I wouldn't have had the strength to leave Istanbul without gazing my fill one last time at Sarayburnu, the Bridge, the lead domes of the mosques, the slender minarets, the Stone Barracks.

We're passing an American armored ship with barbed-wire masts. Near Leander's Tower, before Beşiktaş, all the bends of the Bosporus are packed. The sea of Istanbul is jammed with dreadnoughts, cruisers, torpedo boats, and camouflaged freighters. Wrenched with pain, I had watched this enemy, this insult, this leaden steel horde many times. But now I regard it with confidence in myself. And I don't care that more submarines swim under the sea of Istanbul than mullets, mackerel, and bonitos. I'm off to Anatolia, to Mustafa Kemal Pasha.

I'm in the forecastle steerage, standing amid the crowd of poor men, women, and children with their bundles, baskets, and trunks. I take in my city. Not just one district, one bend or promontory, but the whole city. I know: there, outside the barracks and the armories, the Scots, New Zealanders, and Indians of the British Army stand guard. The puppet soldiers march away from each other, then turn around and again walk up and come face-to-face with each other. I know: this guard ritual is very useful to us. When the guards turn their backs to each other and march away, we jump them—at night, of course— drag them off and enter the depots. If the guards are Indian, especially if they're Muslims, you don't even need knives. They just surrender; some even help. But the sailors, the infantry, the gunners, the French, British, Americans, Italians, Greeks, the soldiers from Madagascar and Australia—when they smash our windows, beat our children, or attack our women, we kill them.

. . .

I walked out the Gülhane Park gates. It's almost evening. The street is empty. An occasional pedestrian or two. All downcast. I stop. A streetcar screeched, turning a corner somewhere. I took a couple steps. Then I saw a woman in a burka run down the street. This is the first time I've seen a covered woman run. It's clear she's being chased, running from someone. She doesn't scream. Her veil is down. She has only one shoe, and she's limping. With my eyes used to sensing what's behind a veil, I can tell she's an older woman. The woman ran past the man walking absent-mindedly down the other side of the street—even today I can vouch that he was a clerk and even that he worked for the Finance Ministry—and stopped when she came up to me.

"Brothers, help me!"

Maybe she said something else. But I clearly heard "brothers" and "help."

Two French soldiers, Foreign Legionnaires, appeared at the head of the street, running and swinging their arms. The woman collapsed at my feet. The Finance clerk across the street walked toward us. A man at the bend down the street looked back; he looked and stayed where he was. The Legionnaires rolling down the street—that's how they seemed to me—came closer. I stepped between them and the woman. One of the soldiers hit me. I reeled. I blacked out or, I mean, I closed my eyes. I heard voices:

"Şinasi, you take the thug on the left."

"Done."

I opened my eyes. The Legionnaires lie flat on their backs.

"Get lost, kid." These words are to me.

"Sister, lean on my arm." This to the woman.

"Effendi, you, too, beat it!" These words to the Finance clerk.

They were three young men; maybe they weren't young, but that's what they looked like to me. I saw their knives. One wiped his on his sash and stuck it back in his pants. They took the woman by the arm and disappeared into Gülhane Park.

We're killing them. They're scared now—not just on the outskirts of the city but in the back streets of Beyoğlu, they're afraid to walk alone, and not just at night but in broad day. I know: their fear makes them crueler. They collaborate with the Sultan's police and raid our houses, and after they torture our people in police stations, they exile those left alive to the deserts of Africa, to islands lost in the ocean. I know: they grow twice as cruel, because we're killing them and smuggling their arms to Anatolia, but I'm not one of those killing them or smuggling arms. I don't know how to kill or to smuggle arms. That's why when Süleyman—we worked at the same paper, where I sometimes did caricatures—proposed we go to Anatolia, I was overjoyed.

It took us seventy-five hours to reach Inebolu.

Inebolu has no pier or breakwater. Ships drop anchor out in the sea, and fishing boats row passengers ashore. In stormy weather, ships don't even stop—they just sail on by.

Inebolu is the first Anatolian town I saw, and it was here that I first saw the Anatolian peasant woman. I saw her in the market place. She squatted against a wall, still loaded with the bundle of wood on her back. I saw her bare feet—they looked like two huge turtles out of their shells. I saw her hands—her sacred hands as they gripped the rope bundling her load of wood, furious as if handling an axe, patient and tender as if rocking a cradle.

Tevfik, Süleyman, and I had been in Inebolu three nights and four days. Tevfik was a poet. Last year he received the Sultan's medal for a poem. And he kept saying on the way: "I hope this medal thing doesn't get me into trouble."

I hear the roar of the Black Sea. The waters of the Bosporus sound different by the pier of the seaside house in Üsküdar, softer and more mysterious. I heard the piercing whistle of a ship, the whistle of the boat they put Süleyman and Tevfik on. Did they lock them in their cabin? Did they throw them in the cargo bilge? Damn it. A kind of despair came over me. And it's spreading fast, turning into a dark shame. I feel like I broke a promise, failed at solidarity, failed to help. At one point I went so far that I felt I was a despicable bastard. I got out of bed. The gas lamp was still on. I put it out. The faint starlight of the night outside glimmered in the room. I sat on Süleyman's bed. It was still warm. But why did they send them right back? Should I have said, "Send me back, too?" Did I sell out my friends? To whom? And am I friends with them? But Süleyman helped me. I'm here thanks to him. If they had sent me back and left them here, what would they have done? I suppose they wouldn't have said anything. To think like this, to search for excuses—isn't this shameful? The wide roar of the Black Sea fills the room. A wind must have kicked up. I stuck my head out the window and smelled the wind—salty, but not like the damp, salt air of the Bosporus; it's soggy salty. I closed the window.

Okay, so they sent Tevfik back because he received a medal from the Sultan. But Süleyman? I'm sure he has nothing to do with the occupying forces. He fled to Anatolia because he was up to his neck in debt.

I couldn't sleep till morning.

Ahmet scratched his neck. His hair had grown too long. I should have Ismail cut it again, he thought.

The next morning, one of the men in breeches came in. We left the hotel. The sea was calm. Caiques lay capsized on the sand beach, and dark children ran around barefooted, shouting and screaming, playing tag among the nets hung out to dry. We went into a room on the first floor of a wooden house. I mean *I* went in; the man who had brought me stayed at the door. Inebolu's Military Police chief—a man in a raincoat and kalpak—showed me to a chair next to his table; it looked attached to the table. I sat down. Crossed my legs. I hated this man the minute I entered the room. I asked him in a rage I could not hide—*would* not hide: "Why'd you send my friends back to Istanbul?"

"I didn't. Orders came from Ankara. They were sent back because they couldn't be trusted."

With the very long, very thin fingers of his right hand—they looked like five hundred, not five—he started drumming on the table. He had fallen quiet after he answered my question in his indifferent voice. And he narrows his eyes. But he's also smiling. I feel he's suspicious of me, but I can't figure out why, why he would be suspicious, and this doubles my rage. I hadn't yet learned there's a place for people who suspect everyone, with or without a cause.

He stood up, leaned over me, and said with the same low, tired voice: "You may leave for Ankara any time you wish. Here's a hundred liras travel allowance."

He laid the money on my knee and straightened up. He was drumming again.

I stood up. The money fell on the floor. I picked it up, crumpled it, and stuffed it into my pants pocket. Maybe because I had to bend over to pick it up, maybe because I hadn't taken money— unless as payment for something—from anyone but my grandfather on holidays, or maybe because this low-voiced stranger I felt suspected me had laid the money on my knee, or maybe because of the gloom of a mess of murky feelings, I felt overcome with a sad revulsion. I left without even saying goodbye.

I walked into the coffeehouse and ordered tea, and the first words I heard—I didn't notice who said them—were: "Those guys they put on the boat last night, they'll dump them in the sea outside Kerempe. Ankara's orders."

I bolted from the coffeehouse. Breathless, I stood before the MP chief: "They're going to dump Süleyman and Tevfik in the sea!"

"Where did you hear that?"

"In the coffeehouse."

"Who from?"

"I don't know."

"Young man, don't worry: your friends will be safely returned to Istanbul."

Again he said it in such a weary, indifferent voice that I wasn't even offended he had called me "young man," and I believed him. And that's how it turned out. Süleyman and Tevfik returned to Istanbul safely. One continued to dodge his creditors; the other wrote another poem to the Sultan. And after the declaration of the Republic, they worked for a paper published by the Ministry of the Interior. Now they're both members of Parliament.

Ahmet fished out the cigarette pack and matches from under his bed. He lit a cigarette. Ismail lightly snored.

With the help of the innkeeper, I hired a mule driver, and the next day at sunup, I left Inebolu. They'd said it would get really cold as we climbed the mountains. My coat was thin—a single-layer. They advised I line my chest, back, and shoes with newspaper. And that's what I did. And I bought a giant kalpak, a gray astrakhan kalpak. The burro was in no condition to carry my suitcase and me. Plus, it was beneath my dignity to ride a donkey.

Inebolu was about three-quarters of an hour behind us. But on the mountain path we were climbing, I could still see below, on my left, both the town and the Black Sea; on my right, the valley; and ahead of me, the snowy mountain range. Summer sun on the Black Sea, spring in the valley, and winter in the mountains. I stopped. "Here it is! Here's my country! Here's my beloved Anatolia!" I caught myself shouting, my right arm thrust forward.

The driver stares at me, confused. I collected myself. And smiled, embarrassed. But this embarrassment left me very quickly. In the same emphatic voice, but this time without thrusting out my arm: "Such beauty," I told the mule driver, "it doesn't exist even in Switzerland!" But I had seen Switzerland only in the little colored pictures that came with Toblerone chocolates.

The driver did not answer.

"Git, boy," he said to his donkey. We pushed on.

I look around at the views right and left and think, "Is anyone in the world happier than me?" but I don't say what I think out loud. For some reason, I'm hesitant before the driver.

We covered a lot of distance. Inebolu and the Black Sea disappeared. At one bend in the road, we ran into eight or ten people resting. They were all from Istanbul; I could tell from their clothing. They all had backpacks like bags or bundles. They were smoking. We talked. They were all reserve officers. Some had fought at Gallipoli, some in Palestine, and some in Galicia. After the war, they went back to Istanbul. One returned from being a POW—all the way from India. Most had been teachers before they went to war. They'd come to Inebolu a week ago. They were on their way to Ankara and then to the western front.

"How old are you?" they asked.

"I just turned nineteen."

"We'll soon see you at the front."

Together, we started walking. One of them, the one back from prison in India, looked sick. We loaded his backpack on the donkey.

At about nightfall in the Ilgaz Mountains, we arrived at the Ecevit Inn, surrounded by huge oaks and hornbeams. In Inebolu I'd heard the innkeeper's butter and honey were famous. I ordered as soon as I sat down on the bench, for both myself and the driver. The lavash bread was steaming hot. The butter melted and blended with the honey. To this day, I haven't eaten anything so incredible. As I drank my kefir, I saw my traveling companions at the other end of the bench eating the bread and cheese they had carried in their packs.

"Why don't you eat this butter and honey?" I asked.

They didn't answer. I offered them the butter, served on grape leaves, and the honey in the wood crock before me. They wouldn't touch it. Before I could decide whether I should say what popped into my head, I said it anyway: "Didn't they give you a travel allowance?"

"They did."

"How much?"

"Ten liras each."

First I was stunned, then ashamed, then angry: "They gave me a hundred liras. You're going to the front; I'm going to paint pictures. But my uncle is a senator in Ankara; that's why they sent me hundred liras. It's a disgrace, damn it. If you want to do me the least favor, let's eat up this money together."

Yes, no, it's embarrassing, and so on. While they debated, the innkeeper brought everyone butter, honey, lavash, and kefir. But I feel an unbearable shame inside me. I'm like a prodigal heir spending his fortune wining and dining the poor.

Damn it. Did I think all this back then? Or am I thinking it all now?

Ahmet sits up in bed in the dark, hugging his knees. The motor hums, filled with longing for home, or calling him away somewhere, calling nonstop. Somewhere far away. "The ship with a hundred masts, where is the port it sails for?"

When we got to Kastamonu, the mule driver said: "You want a woman, effendi? The whores here are famous."

I thought a minute. I want a whore. I want to sleep with an Anatolian woman, even a whore. But I remember Kastamonu is also famous for syphilis. I'm scared, as if I'd gotten syphilis.

"No," I said. "What about you?"

"Not now, but on the way back, God willing, I might stop."

I sat in on the Independence Tribunal in Kastamonu.

"What do you think they'll be sentenced to?"

"Well, they won't hang them, brother!" Ismail said.

"Maybe not, but what'll they get? And maybe they will hang them. I don't know if this is the old prosecutor of the Independence Tribunal in Kastamonu."

Before my eyes, the Independence Tribunal in Kastamonu sentenced a man to fifteen years. Judging by his looks, I'd say he was half-peasant, half-small town. He drank rakı he'd distilled at home. Rakı is prohibited in Anatolia.

My second night in Ankara, my uncle hosted a dinner for his friends in the Assembly. When the bottles of rakı arrived at the table, I asked—not intending to challenge anyone, but just because the words slipped out of my mouth: "I thought rakı was outlawed. Somebody got fifteen years in Kastamonu for drinking rakı."

My uncle laughed: "The prohibition doesn't apply to us."

"But if it's the law?"

"If we applied the law to everyone, we'd all be in a fine mess." I'm not embellishing this conversation with my additions or revisions. This is what my uncle said: "If we applied the law to everyone, we'd all be in a fine mess."

And I also drank the rakı; I didn't even think of not drinking, I drank. And not just that night, either.

Toward the end of the dinner party, a pudgy-faced man I later learned was a big-wheel senator said: "Ahmet Bey, I heard you're a good painter." Where did he hear it? Must have been from my uncle. "If you took a photograph, something monumental, of Mustafa Kemal and enlarged it in oils, I could get you fifty gold pieces from the Pasha. Fifty shining gold coins."

I did not enlarge a picture of Mustafa Kemal. I hated the fifty shining gold coins the pudgy-faced man could get me from the Pasha. If not for those fifty coins, I would happily have taken the job back then.

"Back then," he repeated out loud, "back then."

He suddenly realized how short a time the days "back then" had lasted, and felt strangely sad. He remembered being introduced to Mustafa Kemal in his office at the Assembly building: my heart racing, I saw steel-blue, then gold-yellow, then white hands—shapely, beautiful hands. Maybe this is just how I remember it. Maybe his hands weren't like that, but I'm sure about the blue of his eyes and the gold of his hair.

"Our people are in the hands of the Independence Tribunal. And the bones of the fifteen are off Sürmene, at the bottom of the Black Sea."

Ahmet leaned over to the table and crushed out the cigarette burning his fingers. The motor pounded in the pitch-black cottage *da-dum-dum-da-dum-dum*. Through this roar he tried to hear Ismail breathing. Yes. He's peacefully sleeping. Does he dream about me? Attacking him, shooting him? Ahmet lit another cigarette. He tried not to think about Ismail.

On the Inebolu-Ankara road, we came to a stream. No bridge or anything. I took off my shoes and socks and rolled up my pants to my knees. We'd ended up there because we had tried to take a shortcut. Crossing the stream, I saw, coming from the opposite shore, a peasant—not old, clean-shaven, which means not yet forty—riding a peasant woman across the stream. Crippled, I thought. But when the guy came ashore, he climbed down and walked.

"What's with that?" I asked the mule driver.

"His wife," he said. "He crossed the stream on her back. It means she's a strong woman."

Ahmet smiled. He remembered telling this to Anushka.

It was nightfall. He can't remember if it was before or after Kastamonu. Strange, why can't I remember? I suppose I'll go senile early—if I don't get rabies first. Forget this rabies thing—it was *after* Kastamonu, I remember it very well.

It got dark after Kastamonu. It's almost night, and we're still walking. A God-forsaken wasteland. Not a single tree, not a roof, not a moving shadow. The earth, desolate, extends endlessly in all directions.

"Do we have far to go?"

"The village is here, effendi."

"Where?"

"Under our feet."

In the dark I saw some swellings in the ground. And some holes, some with smoke coming out. Dogs barked underground.

"We're walking on the roofs of the village, effendi."

The village roofs were level with the ground. We walked a few more steps and descended into the village by a path as narrow as a goat's path.

I saw the wounded in this village. In the guesthouse, they lay on the ground, flushed in the red glow of the fire. They lay side by side, on their backs or face down. In bloody, dirty bandages and tattered uniforms. Their faces unshaven. They were silent.

The village headman: "They came one night four days ago. They said they'd leave in the morning. They couldn't. Two died. And we're left with the others. I went into town and reported them. 'We'll take care of it,' they said, but no one has come asking after them."

"Do they have a long way to go?"

"All in different directions."

"Where were they wounded?"

"Who knows where. There's a war with the Greeks now."

The village headman said "There's a war with the Greeks now" as if giving news nobody had heard, distant news that didn't concern him.

I went up to the wounded, greeted them, and wanted to talk. They didn't say anything. My driver: "Let them be, effendi, they're too weak." Then he lifted the head of one of them and turned it toward the fire. "This one's on his way out," he said. "He won't last till morning." He didn't say this in a low voice or anything; he said it out loud, right in the face of the man he still held in his hands.

The wounded soldier lifted his head, the bandages black with blood and earth, out of the driver's hands and tried to straighten up on his elbows but couldn't manage it. I helped him lean against the wall.

"Only God knows that," he said. He said this in a low voice—not a whisper but a low voice.

The driver: "Sure, only God knows. But I worked in a MASH unit in Gallipoli during the war. And, God forgive me, but I also know—you don't look like you'll make morning."

"I'll make it, I will . . ."

He didn't. As the sounds of cocks crowing, dogs barking, and women yelling blended outside, inside he died, wheezing, his back still leaning against the wall. This is how I first saw death.

As we were leaving, one of the wounded asked the driver: "Take a look at me, too. Will I see night?"

The driver peered into his eyes with full concentration: "Your eyes don't have the darkness of death," he said. "Only God knows, but they don't."

On the road I asked the driver: "Is it true the guy didn't have the darkness of death in his eyes, or did you just say that to comfort him?"

"Why would I comfort him? Only God knows, but the guy will live."

On this journey I discovered the art of patching. Peasants were covered in patches of cloth stitched together, all different colors and impossible to imagine together. They were sadder than the rags of Istanbul beggars.

And on this journey I also learned that donkeys and oxen could be starved into skeletons.

The children have swollen bellies.

On the entire journey, I never saw a single peasant woman wearing shoes.

In Ankara, my uncle settled me in Stone Khan. This is Ankara's Pera Palace. I am in a stone room, iron bars on its only window. I calculated: I had paid three-fourths of what was left of my travel allowance for the room. I calculated: the owner of Stone Khan must have become a millionaire in a year or two. I'm shocked. Then I am a sworn enemy of this man.

I ran into a poet from Erzurum in Wells Coffeehouse. I'd known him in Istanbul; now he worked as a court clerk in the Assembly.

The city of Ankara was on the steppe. It had sprung up around a hill out of the blue, for no reason, against all sense. On the peak of the hill sits a fortress. When I look at this fortress at night, I feel a storm, a typhoon in some far-off sea, must have lifted a huge galleon into the air and landed it on these inland rocks.

Apart from the National Assembly, the train station, some of the mosques, and buildings like the Stone Khan, the houses in Ankara are a mixture of wood and mud bricks, mostly whitewashed.

One day, in Wells Coffeehouse, I talked with the Erzurum poet about Ankara's Ahis. The Ahi traditions still survived in various forms, he told me, in many towns and villages in central Anatolia: "The Ahis have set up a kind of craftsman-peasant republic, a kind of Bolshevism."

He suddenly stopped, looked around him, and whispered: "The Bolsheviks supply us with guns and gold, but our side fears the Bolsheviks."

That night, walking by myself through the narrow, winding streets of Ankara, past the ironsmiths, weavers, carpenters, and coppersmiths, I almost heard the sounds of the Bolshevik hammers, looms, and axes of the Ahis and the psalms they sang at their services. I knew that the Bolsheviks were enemies of the rich and friends of the poor. Istanbul papers were full of stories

LIFE'S GOOD, BROTHER

of unimaginable tortures inflicted on Russian noblemen, generals, and merchants. The leftovers of the Bolshevik swords took refuge in Istanbul. But they didn't look at all like they had survived torture. The women were duchesses, at the very least, and the men princes. They owned bars and casinos, pimped out their blond, pink, plump wives, and ran the lottery. And I knew the Allies were also enemies of the Bolsheviks. I had heard of Lenin and seen his photographs in the papers; I'd even enlarged one, a charcoal sketch, not because I liked him or anything but because I was so taken by his boundless forehead, his intelligent almond eyes, and even the tuft of hair on his chin.

One night the Erzurum poet and I went to Kamil's theater, a space converted from a barn or a depot. A kerosene lantern with its sad, bluish light hung at the entrance, a single kerosene lantern. We went in. The audience sat silent on wooden benches, their hands on their knees. But in Istanbul the improvisational theaters, whether in Şehzadebaşı or the Kuşdili fields—the improvisational theaters of Istanbul, indoors or outdoors, are fairgrounds. The people in the audience fast become friends, and those who know one another joke around; the vendors of pistachios, soda, lemonade, and sour-cherry ice cream hawk their stuff, shouting and clacking their plates, glasses, and spoons; the clamor of the band of drums, bells, clarinets, and trumpets outside carries inside the joy and excitement of the blue, red, and green electric lights, the streamers, and the banners at the entrance until the curtain goes up. When the curtain rises and the painted, sequined, plump girls start their flirtatious songs—with their sinuous moves, come-hither looks, and seductive antics—it's total chaos. With people yelling "Hooray! Long live!" or screaming "Sister, I'll eat your tongue!" or shouting "Oy! You're killing me!"—all hell breaks loose. After the singers, the audience plays out the comedy or drama together with the actors. They hiss at the actor playing the villain and give advice to the girl falling into a trap. Between acts, the racket and screams of the vendors, chiming with the band now playing inside, resound throughout the place. The improvisational theaters of Istanbul are fairgrounds. But the one in Ankara was like a funeral home. The audience stared at the curtain, at the angel with his long skirts and trumpet rising toward the torn clouds above; some looked distracted, some sullen, and others bewildered. You can tell the Istanbul people from Ankara natives and the senators from the bureaucrats, but they had one thing in common.

The Erzurum poet whispered: "Fear. Ankara is the city of fear."

I know Othello Kamil from Istanbul—a student trained by the great Armenian actor Papasian. Because he plays Othello even better than his mentor, he's known as "Othello Kamil."

The curtain rose. On stage, wearing a short gold-embroidered jacket, shalwars, and a fez with dangling gold coins, stood a diminutive dark woman. An Armenian from Kayseri, the Erzurum poet said, and I immediately knew that he was in love with her.

The woman stands motionless, with her exquisite mouth, boundless eyes, and thick eyebrows darkened with kohl. A few claps came from the back rows. I turned around to look. The Erzurum poet said: "Workers from the munitions plant."

Imperceptibly, the woman smiled in the direction of the clapping, then started singing, in the most touching voice on earth, "The green frogs chatter on the ponds." The sadness gave me goose bumps. "Alone, orphaned in foreign lands," and once again I crossed the desolation of Anatolia, with its reserve officers from Istanbul and Izmir heading for the front, its wounded soldiers dying in village guesthouses, its women ferrying their men on their backs across streams, its syphilitic whores in the brothels of Kastamonu, its snotty, lice-ridden, barefoot children in sheer rags, the Köroğlu fortresses in

Çamlıbel villages, the wooden plows, the cracked earth—once again I crossed from one end to the other. The pain is unbearable. Damn it!

The woman sang two more songs. The curtain fell and rose. The same woman—same mouth, same eyes with the same kohl-lined eyebrows, and same sorrow—performed a belly dance, clacking wooden spoons in her hennaed hands. The curtain fell and rose. Shakespeare began. The same woman, now in the long skirts of the angel on the curtain and with fake white flowers in her black hair, became Desdemona. Kamil was again wonderful as Othello. All the players improvised. Only Kamil recited the full text. And Iago.

After the play, I met Raşid, who played Iago. He had removed his makeup. A redhead with an amazingly freckled face, he was a small, youngish man. His round, hazel eyes are jumpy, his voice sticky-sweet. Offstage, he still speaks in Iago's voice. He was a graduate of Robert College in Istanbul. And his French was supposed to be as good as his English.

"I know all of Shakespeare by heart," he said. "And the sonnets, too."

He's the son of a retired ambassador.

"Shakespeare's theater," he said, "was bigger than ours, but it had something in common with ours. Here, in Ankara, when I step onto that wooden platform, I feel like I'm in Elizabethan London. Let's get together, Ahmet Bey. I'm at Stone Khan. You haven't noticed me, but I noticed you long ago. I'd heard your name in Istanbul, too."

I was surprised he knew my name. Maybe from my caricatures, I thought.

"If you'd be kind enough to wait a minute, we can walk back to Stone Khan together, Ahmet Bey."

The Erzurum poet said: "We have to stop somewhere first."

"As you wish."

Raşid turned to me: "Let's get together, Ahmet Bey."

Walking back, the Erzurum poet said: "Don't get friendly with that guy. Who knows what he is. Anyway, in Ankara, don't talk to people you don't know."

The streets were pitch-black. We passed patrolmen.

"Ankara is a Noah's Ark," said the Erzurum poet, "a Noah's Ark floating on the deluge of the collapsed Ottoman Empire. Certainly, it will reach safe haven with its doves, snakes, lions, tigers, wolves, and lambs all side by side; it will reach safe haven, and there the snakes will eat the doves, the wolves the lambs. The lions and tigers will fight it out, at one another's throats."

The coffeehouses had long closed. We came to Haymarket.

"This is where they hanged the British spy Mustafa Sagir," he said.

As we parted at the door of the inn, he repeated: "Don't get friendly with Raşid. You never know, do you understand?"

"I understand."

Mustafa Kemal Pasha lives outside the city, protected by his Laz guards.

The western front is both too close and too far away. They say that the cannon fire in the Second İnönü Battle, which began on March 23 and ended on March 31, could be heard in Ankara. I don't know if it's true, but when the Greek army started marching toward Ankara, they say the government officials and the wealthy fled Ankara on trains, in carriages, and on ox-carts and moved farther inland. After the Greeks "abandoned the battlefield to our forces" and retreated, some returned to Ankara while others moved on to Sivas.

The most fertile soil of Anatolia, its most skilled cities, are in enemy hands: fifteen provinces and townships, nine big cities, seven lakes and eleven rivers, three seas and six railroads, and millions of people, our people, are in enemy hands.

I saw my uncle: "I want to go to the front."

"Impossible," he said.

I insisted.

"I'll see," he said.

When we met three days later, he said, as if giving great news, "I spoke with people—he didn't say with whom but made it clear he had spoken with people high in the government, perhaps at the very top—"you do not have permission to go to the front. They'll find you a job in the Press Office."

I did not try to fathom why I was not permitted to go to the front. Maybe I could have insisted on going, and maybe I would have been allowed, but I didn't.

"I don't want to work for the Press Office. Find me a teaching job in some town," I said.

He looked at me the way a smart man looks at a fool, and a week later I set out for Bolu, again on foot, my suitcase again on the back of a mule. My mule driver was lame.

THE FIFTEENTH LINE

ONCE AGAIN, Ahmet read from cover to cover the book of poems Ziya had left. Who knows how many times he'd read it. He poured water on the ground. Tried to make a mud figurine. First, he tried to make Anushka's head, but couldn't. Then he tried a cat. It didn't work out. Then he tried to write a poem. He didn't know how or what to write. He'd never figured out *aruz* meters anyway. Plus, who writes in *aruz* any more? He tried to write in syllabics, with seven-seven stops. In the measure of "The ship with a hundred masts, where is the port it sails for?" "Distance is the thorny briar; you, my rose, are its bitter fruit." Although there are many rhymes for "fruit," none of them helped a second line emerge. If I were a poet, I told Anushka, I wouldn't write love poems. How did it pop into my head to write a poem? "The ways of this sluttish world . . ." Why is the world "sluttish"? The world is beautiful. What does it mean to say "the world is beautiful"? What's beautiful about the world? For what percentage of people is the world beautiful? The great majority of people don't even ask whether the world is beautiful. As if injustice, hunger, tyranny, or death didn't exist, they live with injustice, hunger, tyranny, and death. What percentage of people fight against injustice and tyranny? So we fight. The masses that make revolutions and put up barricades fight. Am I not fighting? By waiting to turn rabid and be shot dead by Ismail's bullet? Damn it!

THE SIXTEENTH LINE

THE BOLU TREASURER was replaced. The Bolu schoolteach-ers, who hadn't been paid for months, decided, at Ahmet's instigation, to meet with the new treasurer, present their dire situation, and, if necessary, hand him an ultimatum. Their elected representatives gathered on a Thursday afternoon in Mirror Coffeehouse and set out for the Town Hall, all worked up and in a fury. Ahmet and the religion teacher, Şaban Effendi from Rumelia, up in front, with the math, history, and litera-ture teachers following, they marched through the market-place. It was raining. One umbrella up front, and three behind, marched on. Ahmet didn't have an umbrella. The shopkeep-ers greeted the furious delegation of umbrellas with hope and respect. All the teachers, including Ahmet, owed the shopkeepers money. The marketplace knew why they were off to see the treasurer.

They turned the corner. The rain got heavier. Ahmet turned back to look. The three umbrellas were down to two.

"Where's the literature teacher?"

The history teacher answered: "He stopped in the market to buy cigarettes. He'll catch up."

The religion teacher, Şaban Effendi, grumbled: "Good God! Is this any time to buy cigarettes?"

One umbrella ahead and two behind, they entered the Gardens. A woman in a soaked black burka, without a veil, saw the men coming. She turned her face to a garden wall and squatted down while they passed. The Gardens behind them, they entered a muddy field. Ahmet again turned back to look. The two umbrellas behind were down to one.

"Now where's the history teacher?"

The math teacher answered: "He had to piss."

The religion teacher, Şaban Effendi, grumbled: "That's CUP people for you. They have to piss at the oddest times." The math teacher belonged to the old CUP party.

The rain came down in buckets. Ahmet took cover under the umbrella of the religion teacher. As they entered the Town Hall, Ahmet turned to look back. There were no umbrellas behind them. As Şaban Effendi folded his umbrella on the steps, he grumbled: "It's your fault, Ahmet Bey. Why involve such people in something so important?"

Ahmet asked the doorkeeper outside the treasurer's office door, heavy as a mosque's: "Tell the treasurer the Bolu teachers are here to see him."

The doorkeeper left and came back.

"Go on in," he said.

Ahmet lifted the heavy drapery and walked in. The treasurer was seated at his table: black eyes, black kalpak, heavy build.

Ahmet: "We, the religion teacher, Şaban Effendi, and I . . ."

The treasurer raised his hand and cut him off: "I see you, but where is the religion teacher?"

Ahmet turned to look back. Şaban Effendi was gone. Ahmet was furious: "Şaban Effendi is outside your door. Ask him to come in."

"No need."

"Five of us started out, only I . . ."

"You're the one I need. Sit down."

"Our salaries . . ."

"I gave the orders. You'll get a month's pay."

"But we . . ."

The treasurer again raised his hand to interrupt Ahmet and rang the bell. He ordered the doorman to get tea, and said:

"Tell the hodja effendi outside not to wait."

The doorman left. The treasurer got up and stood before Ahmet. "Ahmet Bey," he said. "I know who you are, your beliefs, your activities in the town and the villages. And your friends, likewise. The criminal court judge Yusuf Bey, the accountant Osman Bey—all your followers."

He fell quiet. Then he put his big hand on Ahmet's knee and slowly continued: "The Greek army is advancing on Ankara."

"What're you saying? Again?"

"Ankara may fall."

"Ankara may fall? If Ankara falls?"

"We will declare Bolshevism here."

"Bolshevism?"

"You'll make me president. We'll form an army and liberate Ankara. Get your people ready. But, for now, don't tell anyone about me."

Ahmet stared at the treasurer as if just whacked on the head with a bat. He understood some things but not others. The treasurer, his hand still on Ahmet's knee: "Talk to Yusuf Bey and Osman Bey about my proposal. You can take over the Department of the Interior, Osman Bey the Treasury, and Yusuf Bey will be Prime Minister."

Ahmet suddenly snapped out of his daze. He's listening, relaxed, and understands everything. The doorman brought the tea and left. The treasurer, slowly stirring in his sugar, mentioned the Guard commander and the police chief. He said the former could be won over, but the latter should absolutely not be trusted.

When Ahmet left the treasurer, his head was crystal-clear. As he went down the steps, he thought over who could be trusted among the teachers, the young group. The backward faction: the Turkish teacher, the phys. ed., physics, and chemistry teachers. In the youth camp, the municipal engineer and his friends. In the villages, all the poor people. In the market, the coppersmith Ferhat and his friends.

The rain had stopped. I looked for Osman and Yusuf but couldn't find them. Where are they, damn it? I went to the coffeehouse, where the delegates greeted me, agitated and embarrassed.

"We'll get our salaries," I said, and I bolted out of there without asking anyone why they'd all abandoned me halfway.

Osman and Yusuf still aren't where they should be. Where are they, damn it?

Yusuf sits on the Bolu Criminal Court. The other members and the prosecutor are all both very lazy and very old. The Criminal Court is in Yusuf's hands. I teach art at the Bolu Middle School. Osman, Alyanak Osman Bey, works as the accountant of the Agriculture Bank in Bolu. He was in Germany between 1915 and '19. I first heard of Marx from him, but only the name and the words "Workers of the world, unite!" And that he had said, "History is class warfare." But because we were taught history as the stories of padishahs and kings, I took this to mean "History is warfare between padishahs and kings," and I thought this was absolutely right. Who-knows-what padishah fights with who-knows-what king, and the people are crushed in the fray. But now history wasn't going to be like that: we're getting rid of the padishahs, and wars along with them.

Actually, the Bolu Criminal Court has two members: Yusuf and Osman. And the real prosecutor is me. They glance over the cases in the courtroom. The decisions are really made at the Mulers' Inn, at night, in my room above the stables. We only ask if the defendant is rich or poor and whom he offended. If he's poor and offended a rich man: acquittal. If he's rich, even if innocent: a sentence. We open the law books only when a poor man is accused of a crime against another poor man, or a rich man is accused of a crime against another rich man. In the villages and the town, the fame of the Criminal Court— or, really, of Yusuf—had spread far and wide among the poor people. And Alyanak Osman Bey had all sorts of tricks to make poor people's debts to the bank either disappear from the books or be slashed. And at school, I seat the children of the poor in the front row and, whether they can draw or not, give them top grades. And then there was the Youth Club, and we got them on our side, too.

In my room above the stables of the Mulers' Inn, above the neighing, the clanging chains, and the smell of manure, and by the light of a gas lamp, I told Yusuf and Osman what the treasurer had said. We spoke with the treasurer twice. We made plans. But Ankara did not fall. The treasurer called us in again: "There's nothing left for you to do here. Now go away—don't get me in trouble," he said. About that time, Yusuf got a telegram, I don't know from whom. But he said, "They're sending me to Trabzon on some business. This is an opportunity—you come, too. Then we'll all go to Russia together and learn what Bolshevism is really all about."

We accepted Yusuf's proposal. He left, but Osman returned to Istanbul. And I set out for Trabzon.

I didn't find Yusuf at the Trabzon address he'd given me. The owners of the house where he'd been staying suggested a coffee-house: "Sometimes he went there to play backgammon. The backgammon master, Hafız, goes there, too." I went to the coffee-house: "Yusuf Effendi hasn't been here for many days," they said. I returned to the hotel. Couldn't sleep. Came downstairs to step outside, and met the innkeeper.

"Where are you off to, effendi?"

"I couldn't sleep."

"It's late—the coffeehouses will be closed."

"I'm not going to a coffeehouse. I just want to walk around and get some fresh air."

"You know best, but it's very late."

I was taken aback.

"What, do they mug people here?"

"No. But . . ."

"But what?"

"You just came to Trabzon today; you're a stranger here."

"So?"

"Nothing, but after the trouble, they're watching strangers."

"What trouble?"

The innkeeper didn't answer. It's clear he's sorry he said anything.

"What trouble?"

"If you must walk around, bey, walk around. But I took a liking to you, that's all—but you know best."

I went back to my room. I lifted the cotton curtain of the room and looked out: the late-night dark of all Anatolian towns.

I left the hotel early the next morning and went back to the coffeehouse. The waiter was hosing down the sidewalk. A couple of customers were inside. The owner recognized me: "Yesterday, after you left, Yusuf Effendi came in. I told him. A young man, I said, a young man in a peaked kalpak, asked after you. You didn't tell me your name. I said he looked like he was from Istanbul, with long sideburns—like this."

"What did Yusuf say?"

"First, he didn't know. Then, 'Oh, I know him,' he said."

"And?"

"He didn't say anything more."

"What do you mean he didn't say anything more? Didn't he say I should wait for him if I come in tomorrow?"

"He didn't. But you can wait if you like. Today the shah of backgammon players, Hafız, will be coming in. Yusuf Effendi will probably come in, too."

I don't understand. But I can do nothing but wait. "Are there frequent boats to Batum from here?"

He looked at me with a strange expression: "Yes, from time to time."

"There must be small boats, motorboats and so on."

"Sure."

The coffeehouse owner went away and returned with tea, a sesame bagel, and cheese.

"On your way to Batum?"

"Kars, by way of Batum—through Tbilisi."

This was our plan. At that time, you could reach Kars from Trabzon in two ways. One: overland. The other: sail to Batum, then go down to Tbilisi and Kars. But we're staying in Batum, not going down.

"Do you have a travel permit to Batum?"

"Yes."

I'd had the treasurer in Bolu draw up the papers: "Certificate of official permission to proceed to Kars via Batum-Tbilisi."

"Good. The overland journey is both long and hard. Did you get the permit here?"

"No."

"In Ankara?"

"Bolu."

"Bolu's forms aren't valid here. You'll need to get a permit here, too."

"Won't they give me a permit?"

"God only knows."

The coffeehouse owner walked away. I noticed the customers who had been eavesdropping on our conversation whispered among themselves afterwards.

I ordered another tea. Again, the owner brought it, not the waiter.

"I hear you had some trouble here," I said.

"What trouble?"

"I don't know. The guy at the hotel said something."

For some reason, following a defensive instinct, I didn't name the hotel. I gave the name of another hotel I had passed on my way to the coffeehouse.

"So you don't know about the trouble here?"

"I haven't heard anything."

It was clear he knew.

That day, I waited for Yusuf till dark. He didn't come in.

The next morning, I was back at the coffeehouse: "Did he come in?"

"He came by as I was lowering the shutters."

"And?"

"He said you should wait for him this morning."

A little later, Yusuf walked in. We hugged—I mean, *I* hugged *him*.

"Let's go," he said.

We left.

"Yusuf, what are you up to?"

"Be quiet. I'll explain everything."

"What's happening?"

"I said to be quiet."

We're walking fast. Yusuf, trying not to let on, keeps turning back to look. We're walking really fast. We embark on the narrow, hilly roads of a neighborhood I later learn is called the "Tekke" quarter. He slows down.

"Let's hear it, Yusuf Effendi."

"I had to leave that house."

"Okay, but why didn't you tell the owners where I could find you?"

"I couldn't."

"What do you mean, you couldn't? How was I supposed to find you in huge Trabzon?"

"You found me. Did you say anything to the coffeehouse owner?"

"Like what?"

"I don't know, something thoughtless. You'll say anything."

"I asked about boats to Batum."

"Fine shit."

"Why?"

"You can't travel to Batum with your papers from Bolu. What else did you tell him?"

"I didn't tell him anything else."

"Have the Military Police called you in?"

"No. But how are we going to get to Batum?" Then I suddenly remembered. "Wait, the governor here—my grandfather trained him. I'll go to him for our permits."

Yusuf thought: "Not a bad idea."

I didn't think to ask Yusuf what he was doing in Trabzon.

"You get your papers in order, Ahmet. If you try to get permits for both of us, it'll attract attention. I'll find a way and follow in three or four months. And we shouldn't be seen here together again."

"What's going on?"

"Did you talk to anyone here about Bolu court cases or the treasurer?"

"Who do I know here to talk to?"

"You never know; you're such a blabbermouth."

"Where's that coming from? You're afraid of something, Yusuf. Are you mixed up in something here? And say, something's happened here."

"Who told you?"

"The innkeeper. I asked the coffeehouse man, too."

"Fine shit."

He looked behind him.

"Why do you keep looking back?"

"To see if we're being followed."

"Why would we be followed?"

"You think the Military Police don't know the shit we were mixed up with in Bolu? Listen to me good, Ahmet"—he lowered his voice—"they killed Mustafa Suphi and his men."

"Who are Mustafa Suphi and his men?"

"Turkish Bolsheviks."

"Where, how? Why'd they kill them?"

"Because they were Bolsheviks."

We had come to a hill of pine trees. Yusuf: "Mustafa Kemal invited them from Russia. Suphi was taken prisoner in Russia, then joined the Bolsheviks. Some of his men were from Istanbul. A Congress was held in Baku; that's why they went there."

"And then?"

"When they got the invitation from Mustafa Kemal, they came here. Kazım Karabekir Pasha welcomed them."

We sat under the pines. The weather is wonderful, with a soft breeze off the Black Sea.

"In Erzurum, they had set up—for the hadjis and hodjas, for all the stray dogs— something called 'The Society for the Preservation of Matters Sacred.' They started hooting and throwing stones at the carriages of the Suphis at the city gates, shouting, 'They'll turn our mosques into barns for donkeys! They'll bare our women's heads! They'll make us wear *hats*!' And Karabekir disarmed the Suphis and sent them on to Trabzon."

The Black Sea stretches out empty as far as you can see into the distance: right, left, and straight ahead. No ship's smoke, not a sail.

"Here, one night in Millstream, they put them on a motorboat. January 28. An overseer here, Yahya, was head of the boatmen— a real son of a bitch. One of "Lame" Osman's men. After Suphi's motorboat pulled out, Yahya's men set out on another boat. They pulled abreast of the first boat off Sürmene. They say it had fifteen Suphis on board. And Suphi himself had brought along his wife, a Russian woman. They say the fight lasted about two hours. At some point, Suphi got hold of a gun. He's about to fire, and one of the Trabzon dogs, a bastard by the name of Faik, shot Suphi in the back—in the neck. Then they knifed and strangled the others, chained stones to their feet, and threw them overboard. They took the Russian woman to Trabzon. She was beautiful. She's a prisoner in the overseer's house. Ankara is still scared of what might happen here over this trouble."

"Are there any of us in Trabzon?"

"I don't know. The MPs are on alert."

The Black Sea still stretches out, still empty, still luminous.

Ahmet waited not three but six months for Yusuf in Batum. Yusuf never appeared. He returned to Istanbul in '24 and went into business. He got rich, went bankrupt, and turned to smuggling. In '34, in Yüksekkaldırımlar in Istanbul, he was shot dead by the police in broad daylight.

· · ·

I first saw a picture of Mustafa Suphi: pince-nez glasses, bristly mustache. In Moscow, I blew it up in three or four charcoal sketches. He was one of the men I most respected—more important, loved most—in the whole world.

I'm walking around the park in Batum. Hungry. I have a couple million rubles. I sold my suitcase last week. I thought it was leather, but it turned out to be oilcloth. If I order a glass of tea in the teahouse by the movie theater, not with saccharin but with real sugar . . . I hear the din of the sea. I don't have it in me to gawk at the women sunbathing in the nude.

I was on the beach last night. It was cloudy. In the warm dark, the sea was still, with phosphorescent sparkles. Mustafa Suphi's murder weighs on my mind. As the boat taking me to Batum sailed off Sürmene, I looked at the shore across: green hills, a sand beach, and little houses in the dawning light. An ordinary coastline of our Black Sea coast. Suphi's boat came to these shores in the night, and they only saw the glittering shards of light. Maybe they didn't see them. Maybe a snowstorm raged. Was the sea calm or rough? The crew of the motorboat knew their passengers would be killed. Knowing this, did they speak with them as if nothing would happen? Maybe they offered them tobacco; maybe they lit their cigarettes with their own. What did Suphi's men say among themselves? Did they imagine they could be killed? Or did they somehow sense it? When? When they took away their guns in the State House in Erzurum? Or maybe they got suspicious when their carriages were stoned at the gates of Erzurum. When Kazım Karabekir Pasha talked with the people whose murder he had mapped out like a battle plan, did he snicker to himself? Now I know: the pasha won his campaign against the Armenian Tashnaks with the help of the regiment Mustafa Suphi had assembled from Turkish prisoners in Russia. For the rest of his life the pasha would boast of this victory, which he owed to Mustafa Suphi and his comrades—the very men he sent to their deaths off Trabzon.

Were the Suphis imprisoned when they arrived in Trabzon? I don't know. If they were imprisoned, they must have sensed they'd be killed. But if they weren't? What did they think when they saw the boat coming at them fast off Sürmene? Did they think it was on its way to Batum to get ammunition? Or did the motorboat behind them suddenly appear broadside, out of a snow cloud? But they must have heard its noise. Maybe they couldn't hear it, over the roar of the waves and their own engines. Did they think, "Orders came from Ankara, they will apologize and invite us back"? Or did they see their death coming? They were the best our people had raised—the smartest, most courageous, most Turkish. Our land, the people who live in it, half-hungry, shivering with malaria, going blind with trachoma, dressed in rags, plowing their stony fields with their starving oxen, and after four years of spilling their blood, covered with lice, still going back to fight on new fronts; who loved these, my people, as much as they did? Who among us believed in all that's beautiful, good, and hopeful in people more than they did?

I can see Suphi's face—but only his, the others are blurry. I see the chests, necks, and backs of those who will be killed, but their faces are in a fog. I see the hands, shotguns, pistols, knives, and ropes of those who'll do the killing, even their lips frozen under their mustaches. I see the pistol in the hand of Faik—one of the Trabzon dogs—I see his face, too: hawk-nosed, dark-skinned. And I see his hand. He fires and hits Suphi in the neck. I see the shotgun drop from Suphi's hand. Suphi is pitched overboard. But maybe he wasn't, maybe he dropped to the deck and they chained his feet—right here. Here, now, they're dumping him into the sea. Before the others. The others: I know the name of one of them—Nejat. From Istanbul. A teacher. Is the motor on the boat still running? I can't picture with my eyes how, for two hours, bare hands—hands that don't know how to kill— fought with hands that do, hands armed with knives, shotguns, pistols, and ropes. I don't see the face of Nejat from Istanbul, just his neck. The stone is tied around his neck with a rope. They dumped Nejat overboard. Maybe he was still alive, just wounded, and could see the lights glittering on the opposite shore; I heard the swish of the dark sea, opening and closing. I hear it now. It opened and closed fifteen times.

I'm in the park in Batum. Among the trees, the pond shimmers in the sun. Someone touches my shoulder. I turn around: Raşid. I'm surprised. He hugs me. Raşid, who played Iago in *Othello* in Kamil's theater in Ankara.

"What're you doing here?" I asked.

"I joined the Bolsheviks," he said. "The whole world will turn Bolshevik."

He didn't ask me what I was doing here, and he wasn't surprised to see me. He gave me the address of his hotel. I didn't tell him I was at the Hôtel de France, but a week later he appeared in our room. I'm working for the paper, he said. I introduced him to the members of the Foreign Bureau of the Turkish Communist Party. He left. He returned a month later. I'm the editor of the paper, he said. Batum is the capital of the Soviet Socialist Republic of Adjara. Most Adjarans are Muslims. They speak Turkish and publish a Turkish newspaper. Raşid edited that paper. And we ourselves were publishing a journal, *Red Syndicate*, and shipping it to Anatolia and Istanbul on Laz boats.

The night Raşid last stopped by, the official seal of the director of the Foreign Bureau disappeared. His seal was locked in the drawer of the table. The lock was broken. I'd left the room with Raşid and come back three or four hours later. The window to the balcony had been jimmied open from the outside. We reported the incident to Cheka, and the next morning they called me in. Behind a wooden desk sat a man with a black mustache and glasses—again, pince-nez. He spoke Turkish with an Azeri accent.

"You did not steal the seal," he said. "No need to steal. It was under your hand all the time. Who do you suspect?"

"I don't suspect anyone."

"Your grandfather was a pasha. Your father is a high-ranking bureaucrat. Engels was an industrialist. Mustafa Suphi's father was also a pasha."

"You look like Comrade Mustafa Suphi."

"I look like a good man," he said, smiling.

If he had said, "I look like a great revolutionary, a martyred comrade, a fearless Bolshevik," I would have understood, but I was surprised that he said "I look like a good man"—an "agreeable man."

Spring showers pour down on Moscow. I'm drawing my tenth or seventeenth cat. Si-Ya-U says, "Anushka is coming for tea tonight." "Is there any money," I ask, "to buy stuff?" He has a little, but not enough for even a couple of cakes, and I don't have a cent. I borrow money from the woman custodian, and Si-Ya-U goes shopping.

Anushka and I were intimate, but that did not at all disturb the bond, the strange bond, she had with Si-Ya-U. If I were Si-Ya-U, I would have avoided seeing the girl at all costs.

Raşid entered the room with a huge, bulging briefcase of documents under his arm. On his head sat one of the caps worn by Russian workers. Under his jacket he wore a thin Caucasian belt hung with dangling silver ornaments. "I came for the Convention," he said, "of Education Workers." He was now Adjara's Commissioner of Education.

Anushka came in. I introduced her to Raşid. She liked my cat drawing.

"But that's enough. You know I can't turn around in my room—it's overrun with cats."

We made tea. After Raşid left, Anushka and I went out. The rain had stopped. Anushka took my arm. "Let me stay with you tonight," I begged. She wouldn't let me.

"Why? You let me last night. Why not tonight?"

"I don't know, that's just the way it is . . . "

We kissed under the garden archway. As we parted, she said, "I didn't like the Adjara Commissioner of Education."

"Why not?"

"I don't know, that's just how it goes. Cats like some people right away, but others . . . "

"You're not a cat. A person has a mind and consciousness—especially a Communist. If I were a poet, I wouldn't use the word 'heart.'"

"Do you love me with your head?"

"If I were a poet, I wouldn't write love poems."

Walking home, Ahmet caught himself repeating, "Listen to the flute's lament, it grieves its separation."

Two months later they arrested Raşid as a British spy. As he tried to take refuge in the Turkish Embassy, he was turned away at the door. Ahmet recalled the business about the seal in Batum. He didn't tell Anushka about Raşid's arrest. They exiled Raşid to Siberia. He escaped, returned to Istanbul in '29, and wrote columns like "How I Became a Bolshevik Commissioner of Education" for a paper. He worked for Homeland Security.

THE TWENTIETH LINE

AHMET WOKE UP with a headache. Ismail had left the door partly
open on his way out. Every time, Ahmet jumps out of bed, closes
the door, and lights the lamp. This morning, he didn't move. He
sees the light through the door. The motor pounds *dum-dum-da-
dum-dum* inside his brain. Has it begun? Is this headache *that*
headache? The twentieth day. He reaches for the book on the
chair. It doesn't say which day the headaches start. He strikes a
match and brings it up close to his eyes, practically singeing his
eyelashes: he can look at the flame. But it's still too early: fear
of fire won't start on the twentieth day. He checked the book. It
doesn't say which day it starts. He got up and took an aspirin. He
doesn't feel like eating. Lack of appetite. He made tea and drank
the tea with pleasure. That made him happy, but he still had a
splitting headache. Another aspirin. He closed the door, lit the
lamp, and brought it up to his nose. Normal. He made his bed,
then looked at the lines on the door: all about the same length
and width. He wanted to draw the twentieth line but changed
his mind. Wait till night. What's the hurry? He draws a cat on a
newspaper, then tears it up. He keeps repeating, "The ship with a
hundred masts, where is the port it sails for?"

Let's start our game. Weren't we going to stop this game?
Today is the last time. He sat on the chair. Like Rodin's *Thinker*,
but not naked. He's trying to grab onto what's passing through
his mind. The things that run through your mind—overlap-
ping, entangled, side by side, thick and thin, long and short—
sometimes beget one another, but other times something in no
way related to the crowd inside drops in, comes between things,
then branches out and spreads all over. Once you're caught in
this game, your path is clear all the way to insanity. One of the

rules of the game is that what you can catch going through your mind, what you can grab onto, you must say out loud. You can catch and say only about one percent. The dreams we think we see for hours actually take an instant. Did I read this somewhere, or am I making it up? My headache feels better. To howl like a dog, you must lose consciousness. Stop this shit. I must think something else. I'm thinking in an orderly way. What am I thinking? That I'm thinking in an orderly way. I'm thinking what I'm thinking. I'm thinking what goes through my mind. "What goes through my mind" is the only thing that goes through my mind. The papers stuffed into the cracks in the door. The gun. Where does Ismail stash the gun? Mustafa Suphi with a gun at his neck . . . Now my head really aches. There's a beauty spot on Anushka's left breast. The lamp wick. Why didn't I look up Yusuf in Istanbul? What good would that have done? I came face to face with Alyanak Osman Bey in Beyoğlu, but he looked away and walked on by. Is my head aching or not? Maybe Raşid died in Siberia.

Ahmet stood up. He started reading the novel Ismail brought yesterday. He looked at the clock: ten minutes to lunch. He eats lunch at quarter past twelve, on the dot.

The Twenty-First Line

"My mother's here, Ahmet."

"When? Where? Wonderful."

"At lunch I looked up, and there she stood, waiting by the door. I put her in a hotel. I came here to let you know so you wouldn't worry. I'll be back in two or three hours. I told her I slept in a dorm. My dear mother, I wish you could meet her. It's impossible, obviously, but you should just see her. My mother is one of those mothers in stories and novels. I'll tell you later. I stopped by the hotel after work and told her I'd be right back."

"Don't keep her waiting."

"I didn't tell you anything about my mother. I never talk to anyone about my mother. If I fell in love with somebody, I wouldn't talk about her, either."

"Is that shot aimed at me?"

"No, brother, everyone is different."

"Stop babbling and get moving."

"My mother is one of those mothers in stories and novels. She gave her all—she worked in a laundry and sewed army uniforms—to put me through technical school."

Ahmet didn't ask, "Where was your father? Why did your mother take care of you? What happened to your father?"

"Don't keep the woman waiting."

"I'm going, I'm going. If you could see her, and she's so tiny."

Ahmet didn't ask, "Where's your mother from? What does she do now, who does she live with?"

"She'll stay three or four days. Don't wait up for me; go to bed."

"Beat it!"

Ismail did something he'd never done: he hugged Ahmet. And left. Ahmet put out the lamp and left the door ajar. He could see the stars.

Ahmet realized that he hadn't once thought of his mother in months. He was sorry. My mother didn't give her all; she didn't work in a laundry. Don't I love my mother as much as Ismail loves his? My mother is beautiful.

"On my mother's side, Anushka, the women are all one more beautiful than the next."

"You must have taken after your father."

"True . . . Hey, girl, wait, my mother must be about forty now."

In Strastnoi square, on the bench under Pushkin's statue, we're sitting in the sun. It's Sunday.

"What's your mother's name?"

"Güzide."

"Giuzide."

"Not Giuzide, Güzide. You just can't handle that *ü*."

"And you can't say *ts*."

"My mother writes poems in French."

"Love poems?"

"Nonsense. She's married, a grown woman."

"So?"

"What do you mean, 'So'? Is she going to write love poems to my father?"

"Why to your father?"

"Then to who? My mother plays Beethoven on the piano. My father only knows Turkish music. I got sick at boarding school. They put me in the infirmary. My mother came. She took off her veil. The doctor and the History teacher were both there. I snapped, "Cover your face!" I've been desperately jealous of my mother since I was a child."

Petrosian, the Party cell secretary, appeared across the way. He was distracted. He's eating sunflower seeds, spitting out the shells.

"Hello, guys. Look, what I was going to say, Ahmet—I need material on land ownership in Turkey today. I found some stuff, but from you . . ."

"I don't have any material."

"Haven't you ever been to a village there?"

"I have."

"Didn't you study this question in the villages?"

"No."

"Doesn't your party have publications on this topic?"

"I doubt it."

Petrosian looked into Ahmet's face in despair.

"Still, tell me about the villages you've seen."

He gave Anushka a handful of sunflower seeds. He paused, as if he had something more to say, then walked away, singing an Armenian song.

Anushka: "Petrosian—I could have fallen in love with him."

"That's all we need. Why didn't you fall in love with him? Why could you have fallen in love with him? Is he that handsome? Men don't think the men women find handsome are handsome, and women don't think the women men find beautiful are beautiful."

"I could have fallen in love with him, but not because he's handsome—though he certainly is—but because he knows he has only a few months to live yet lives as if he'll never die."

"And after he died, you wouldn't look at another man, right?"

"I don't think I would. But who knows, maybe . . ."

They got up. Ahmet asked: "Where to, Anushka?"

"I'm going home. I have to do a wash."

"Can I come?"

"If you want."

"Should we go to the Meyerhold tomorrow night?"

"Tomorrow night I'm going to the concert with Si-Ya-U."

"Can I come?"

"No."

"Why not?"

"Because the two of us, Si-Ya-U and I, are going together."

Ahmet didn't say anything. Halfway, he parted with Anushka.

"I just remembered I have something to do, too. Next week, our Turkish arts group will be part of a cultural event at some factory. I have to plan for it now."

Ahmet was asleep when Ismail got back. His covers were off; Ismail covered him up. Ziya used to say, "Ismail, your mother is not a mother but a force of nature. But not something huge, like the sea, wind, or fire, something you can see, but like an atom, infinitesimal but at the bottom of everything."

Ismail's mother will die in 1940. There's a prison guard. From Bursa. Very pro-German. Every night, after saying "God bless" and bolting the door from the outside and locking it, he puts his head up to the peephole and calls to Ismail. "Come over here a minute, master," he says. "Hitler bombed London again. The Germans will win the war. Stop being so stubborn. Just say, 'He'll win.'" "He won't win," Ismail will say. "All right, have it your way," the guard will say, and the next night they'll go through the whole thing all over again. Ismail's mother will collapse and die at the feet of this prison guard from Bursa. In the visiting room, behind the wire screen. Tiny, all shriveled up. She will say, "I brought you grape-leaf dolmas, Ismail. They got a little squished between Manisa and here. And give some to the guard effendi, son," and will collapse at the feet of the guard from Bursa.

Ismail pricked up his ears at the sound of the motor. It's skipping. He thought, "One of the pistons is out," then went to sleep.

The Twenty-Second Line

I HAVE GUESTS: some seated on the floor, on the earth, some on cots and chairs, and one even leaning against the wall by the food cupboard. Another stands to the left of the door. I am standing both to the left of the door and by the food cupboard, leaning against the wall; I'm seated both on the floor, the earth, and on cots and chairs; and I'm also walking around, and the gas lamp on the wood table lights up our faces, some from above, some from below, and some from the side. Anushka comes and goes, without opening or closing the door; she slips in and out through the stone walls and the hole we dug, but without opening or closing the trap door, and inside the glass chimney of the lamp she appears in the cottage and disappears, sometimes right next to the wick, sometimes in and out of the flame. Among my guests are those I love like my very life. And those I hate. But none I feel hostile to. I have no animosity toward anyone. Except those who killed Mustafa Suphi and those who had him killed, and also the exploiting classes, not just in Turkey but all around the world: Fascists, imperialists, and the woman who shot at Lenin; Kolchak, Denikin, the blond officer with the big eyes who shot Anushka's father, and reactionary social democrats; the Greek king, Konstantine, and the *Averof* and the Greek army that torched Izmir, and the Allied navy, the looming silver-colored steel hulls we sailed past to escape Istanbul—I think that's all. I may have overlooked some things.

I have no hostility to anyone else. Sure, the people I count as my enemies also consider me—that is, those who know I'm alive—their enemy. But imperialism, for instance, hasn't heard of me yet. I also feel hostile to people out of the blue. Why? That's just the way it is—as Anushka says, that's just how it goes. Some people are my enemies, but I'm not theirs. Knowing someone is your enemy but feeling no enmity for him—or forcing yourself to say, "I must also become his enemy" and then forgetting about it after a while—is strange. That doesn't quite convey the feeling, but I can't think of a better way of saying it.

I have guests: all the cities I've known, and those I've visited only in books and pictures; all the small towns, mountain roads, forests, streets, nights, days, the trout stream in Kirezli village, Kalamış Bay in Istanbul, wood-paved Tverskoy Boulevard in Moscow, Mirror Coffeehouse in Bolu. I see myself in the mirror across from me, just as I saw myself in Uncle Şükrü Bey's mirror the day I arrived in Izmir, but now I don't have a mustache, just a huge, pointed kalpak, my sideburns down to below my earlobes, my eyebrows knit tight. I'd give the whole world to look ten years older. In the mirror I saw the wretch looking back at me, but what a look—silk-embroidered turban, a fringe beard, black eyeliner. I turned around. He grinned. I threw the tea glass before me at his head. My nickname in Bolu became "Crazy Teacher." I think this upped my status in town.

Cevat doesn't have a fringe beard or a silk-embroidered turban or a pederast in him, but something about him reminds me of that guy. The redhead Raşid, the Commissioner of Education in Adjara, was an amateur actor; Cevat worked as a professional actor. He boasts about it. How he ended up in Russia, I don't know. He works for Cheka. How he got into it, I don't know. He's my enemy. Why? I don't know. We're drinking beer with friends in a bar on the Arbat; I'm telling Petrosian about the villages of Bolu. Cevat comes in and sits at our table. He's drunk. He listens to what I'm saying for a while. Then, "Look here," he says, "you're Mustafa Kemal's agent. We have your file. We have your life in our hands. Your life isn't worth a cent." Before I can answer, Petrosian says, "Get out of here, you drunken bum"— not shouting or anything, almost whispering—and takes Cevat by the arm and leads him out, then comes back. "Revolution," he says, "kicks up such a tempest, such surging waves, that even the weeds at the bottom end up floating in to fill our harbor." Three days later I ran into Cevat in front of the Chat Noir movie house. He shook my hand and patted me on the back. "I'll write a play, and you can stage it," he said. "I'll even direct it." Cevat is my enemy. I don't feel any enmity toward him; I just hate him. Clearly, I consider the feeling of enmity to be important, serious, not something to be wasted.

I met Nuri Cemal in Batum. Pointed gray beard. Around fifty. When he was in Turkey, he wrote books about cooperatives and Turkish grammar. During Sultan Abdul Hamid's reign, he was a Young Turk exiled to Africa, to Fezzan. He writes children's verses, one worse than the other. After the Tsarist order collapsed, he came to Baku to do business and met Suphi and joined the Party. They say his beard covers the scar on his chin. I don't know if he has a scar on his chin. He's a womanizer. Like all old men, he chases young women. Maybe not all old men are that way. He knows French, Russian, and Greek. I learned some Marx from him—the theory of "surplus value," for instance. Like me, he doesn't like to wash—I mean, not too much. The bed in our room in the Hôtel de France in Batum is fit for a king, not because of its sheets or quilts (there are no sheets or quilts, just a blanket) but for its size, the mattress, and the box spring—all fit for a king. We've got this bed and a couch. How many times I insisted, "I'll sleep on the couch, you take the bed," but he'd never agree. "Tomorrow, or the day after, we'll return to our country, Ahmet, and we'll meet with hardships, we'll end up in prison, and if in my old age I get used to beds with springs, prison benches will be too hard on me." He used to pull his coat over him and fall asleep on the couch. He even drank his tea without saccharin. We went to Moscow together. He became a teacher at the university. I introduced him to Anushka. Before long, Anushka said, "Your professor declared his love for me. And he speaks so beautifully."

"Could you have loved an old man, Anushka?"

"How old?"

"Thirty-five, forty."

"I could. Even older."

"You mean it?"

"I mean it."

"That's abnormal."

"Why? Look, an old woman loving a young man is really abnormal—or maybe not. What does love have to do with normal or abnormal?"

Nuri Cemal, our professor, went back to Turkey in '28. He worked at the Language Institute. Became a senator. Died at eighty-two.

The night Anushka and Si-Ya-U were going to the concert, I dropped in on Anushka an hour before. Si-Ya-U was already there.

Anushka: "I thought you had something to do."

"I finished it."

We talked about this and that. Si-Ya-U read classic Chinese poems, first in Chinese and then in Russian translation. When it was time for the concert, Anushka said: "We're leaving."

"I'm staying," I said.

"Okay, but on one condition. On the condition that you take a bath. Don't disturb the neighbors—heat the water in the kitchen after things quiet down, and don't make a mess. Wash yourself in a corner. Use the bathrobe in the closet. But first, go home and get clean clothes. Promise?"

"Promise."

They left. I can't believe Si-Ya-U. He knows my relationship with Anushka, but he still doesn't hide that he's madly in love with her. Isn't he a man? I've been sent home to get clean clothes. Out on the boulevards, I kept thinking of Si-Ya-U, and kept thinking of him on my way back. I lay on my back on the divan in Anushka's room. I still thought of Si-Ya-U, but I calmed down. Anushka and Si-Ya-U. Weird things come to mind. In the kitchen, I put the bucket on the gas burner and went back into the room. I took off my clothes and lay back on the divan. When we listen to music, Anushka touches my knee. She must be touching Si-Ya-U's knee now. So what? How "So what?" They'll walk back from the concert, side by side on the abandoned streets. Why does this happen? Damn it. I must have drifted off. I woke up crazed, with boiling water all over me. Anushka stands by the divan, a bucket in her hand.

"Have you lost your mind, girl?"

"Why didn't you wash? You promised. Get up."

Everything—the divan, me—is soaking wet. I'm furious. "That's an outrage, what you did."

"Don't scream! You'll wake the neighbors."

"Both flirt with Si-Ya-U and . . ."

"What did you say?"

"You heard what I said."

"Here are your clean clothes. Get dressed and get out."

Anushka and I ignored each other for a week.

On the wall of our room, starting on one side of the wall and going all the way around to the other side, I've done a photomontage like a streamer about half a meter wide. Anushka and Kerim are taking it in; Si-Ya-U and I stand behind them. The series of photos represents the social orders. To the right of the door, scenes from primitive communal systems; then tribal orders, the age of serfdom, feudalism, capitalism, and so on; on the left of the door, a new social order: International Communism, the unity of all races in a world without borders, governments, or classes, the man of one race and one nation, the race and nation of Communists.

Anushka: "I always think, when everyone speaks the same language, if this language isn't Russian—and why should it be Russian, maybe it'll be Chinese."

Si-Ya-U: "Could be."

Anushka laughed. "You nationalist, you! Maybe it'll be a mixed language, maybe English or an altogether new language, but if this language isn't Russian, how will people really ever know the pleasure of Pushkin?"

Kerim, his yellow eyes and bushy black eyebrows fixed on the photographs, said: "I haven't read Pushkin. It's embarrassing, but my Russian isn't good enough for me to understand him. And what can I do—he's not translated into Turkish. It doesn't enter my mind that Turkish could be the one language, but I think a few big languages will remain. This isn't about language, though. No one will be hungry or unemployed or illiterate. There won't be any bosses, laborers, peasants, police, or guardsmen. Or any fear of you or me. You'll work as you want, eat, drink, read, write, and enjoy life as you wish. This will happen—I just hope it happens soon. Of course, we can't see its exact shape yet, but if we can see a world revolution, that's enough. Everyone is waiting for the German proletariat to say, 'Go!' Master Seyfi works at the munitions plant in Ankara, but he worked about ten years on the docks of Marseille. He always says, 'Just wait, you'll see what the French workers will do.' And the Paris Commune is all before us . . ."

The organization in Ankara sent Kerim to the university. He's my closest friend in Moscow. He's the mortal enemy of two things: cigarettes and lies. He won't let me smoke near him. "You lie only to the enemy; if you lie, even to a woman, even to make her feel good, you're not a man." He met one of Anushka's friends. They were very sweet together, but the girl couldn't make Kerim say—not even once—"I love you very much, Marusa."

"So you don't love me, Kerim?"

"Why wouldn't I love you?"

"Very much?"

"Not very much."

"Why not very much?"

"I don't know. Just not very much. If I loved you very much, I'd *say* very much. But right now I don't love you very much."

Thirty-seven below, Celsius. Late in the day, Kerim and I went to a Turkish bath on a back street off Tverskoy Boulevard. Because they didn't use towels or anything, and we could never get used to being stark naked, we held the huge bath bowls in front of us, tried not to look at each other, and bathed. We stepped out on the Boulevard. It had gotten dark. All the lights were on, and the tram windows had iced up, like the shop windows. Sleds whirred past us, all around. If you spit, it'll freeze before it hits the ground. There's an Anatolian saying: "It's so cold the foxes are shitting copper." Well, it's that cold. People on the street walk as if running, most in felt boots. A woman in front of us slipped and fell. We helped her up. In our army greatcoats and peaked Bodyoni hats—we'd pulled down the sides and buttoned them up—we're still freezing. In the cold, the din of the city clarifies. I showed Kerim a girl across the street: "Look at her. Her cheeks are so red, so beautiful." "Her cheeks are red from the cold," he says, "and her nose looks like a beet."

The city lives another of its winter nights, unaware of the coming catastrophe. Not just Moscow but Paris, New York, Istanbul, Singapore, Beijing—none of the big cities know it. All of them—some now in daylight, some at dawn, some at high noon—all with their griefs, joys, hopes, sorrows, cars, horse carriages, and rickshaws, factories, shops, houses of stone, wood, or cardboard, those going to work or returning home, the workers, the idlers, those sitting in coffee shops, kissing in parks, filling movie houses, those being born or dying, are all living out their lives. Except for a handful of people on earth, no one knows about the earthquake that will hit very soon now, in just five minutes.

We reached the Chat Noir movie house. Somewhere, suddenly, the huge, high, wooden gates of a courtyard flew open.

I can't tell whether it's next to me, ahead of me, or across from me. Trucks and men race through the gates. I hear someone scream. Many must have been screaming, but I thought I heard a single scream. On the lit-up, busy, long boulevard, a single voice, stronger than the night and the cold, cried out: "Lenin is dead!" Then what? I saw everything go to pieces, not as in a time line but all in a blur. And I heard what I heard the same way. Newspapers were snatched from the hands of those running out of the courtyard. A streetcar stopped before me. It emptied instantly. All the streetcars stopped, all empty. I don't hear a thing. An old man is crying: he's taken off his kalpak and pressed it to his heart. And he's bald. Crying. All the sledges stopped, all empty. The movie houses all emptied, crowds rushing out as if from a fire inside. The same with restaurants and houses. People throw themselves on the street. Tverskoy Boulevard is overrun with people pushing and shoving around the newsboys. A streetcar driver sits on the step of his streetcar, weeping. The red-cheeked girl we just saw is crying. Kerim is weeping, a paper in his hand, but I hear nothing. Everything I see happens inside a boundless aquarium. Someone fainted. Another. I see people hugging, crying on one another's shoulder, but without a sound.

Somebody tugged at my arm. I turned to look: a wrinkled old woman, shrunken, her head covered with a shawl. She tugs at my arm, and her toothless mouth says something I don't understand. I bend down. The voice of a six- or seven-year-old girl asks me with the fear of a child, "Is Lenin dead?" I nod. "So he's dead?" I think she'll take out a cross, but she doesn't, and drops my arm: "We're lost." She repeats, "We're lost. We're lost! We're lost!" Her voice grows thicker, louder. It grows and expands, like a genie emerging from a bottle in a fairy tale; then it's suddenly gone, and I hear real sounds. I heard ten people or so, maybe twenty, sobbing on the day we buried my grandfather, and you can imagine a hundred people sobbing together. But a whole city sobbing? You can't listen to that sound more than five or ten minutes. Or you hear it, but to protect your nerves and your sanity, you act out of instinct, not to go insane, and become deaf to it and don't hear that sound but single cries, right and left, behind and before you.

When I got home, they said, "The Communists will stand watch." Si-Ya-U and I didn't stay in our room. The two of us were not enough to dispel our loneliness. We went to the dorm. Everyone is sitting on his bed. No one talks. Someone starts undressing. We look at him, not with hostility or disgust but astonishment. We watch him as if he was performing a very difficult circus act. He goes to bed, pulling his blanket up to his chin. We all stare at him.

Toward morning I stood watch, inside the door, with a shotgun. And I didn't even know how to use it.

They took Lenin to Kolonni Zal.

Trains carry people to Moscow from all corners of the country. The people who want to see Lenin one last time enter Kolonni Zal through one door, view his body, and exit through the other door; the lines stretch beyond the city limits. Huge fires burn on the streets night and day. Night and day, masses of people flock to Kolonni Zal. Ambulances carry the sick and the freezing to hospitals.

The night of the second day, Petrosian appeared: "Ahmet, get dressed fast." We climbed into an open truck—that is, we barely squeezed in. We drove past the throngs of people filling the streets and warming up at the fires and stopped at the rear entrance to Kolonni Zal. As we walked in, Petrosian said: "You will stand watch at Lenin's head for five minutes, representing the university."

The building called Kolonni Zal was the Officers' Club in Tsarist times; I think now it's the Unions' Club. I climbed the back stairs. A funeral march played somewhere. I entered a room all marble, red velvet, and gilt. It was packed with workers, Red Army officers, bearded and beardless peasants, men and women of all ages from all over, and the funeral march continued. Clearly, more than one band played next door. No one talked in the room. How long did I wait? Someone came up. He whispered, "Let's go." Someone opened the door, the funeral march hitting my face like a raging ocean. It is unimaginably bright. I had seen such huge crystal chandeliers only at the Kremlin Palace. In this light, a human flood slowly, slowly drifts by. I move forward with the man who holds me by the arm. First I saw Krupskaya. Before the masses of flowers, she stands in her plain dress, her straight gray hair parted in the middle. Her arms hang down at her sides. Her slightly protruding eyes wide open, she's staring off somewhere.

Then I saw Lenin where she was looking. I saw his forehead, yellow and unbelievably high. The globe itself. Lenin lies on his back, hands crossed on his chest. I saw his Order of the Red Flag medal. He lies on an elevated stand, in an open coffin filled with red flowers. At his head, two people stand guard on each side, and the same at his feet. I took over from a Central Asian. He said something to me as we changed the guard. I didn't respond. A gun in my hand, I stand motionless at Lenin's head. I see Krupskaya, I see Lenin's forehead. The human flood flows past nonstop, like four rivers: two on the right, two on the left. Most have stopped crying. Those who approach Lenin pass as if blindfolded, then suddenly stop as if they've bumped into something, and then, pressured by those behind them, proceed, and until they leave the hall they keep turning back to look, even though they can no longer see him. I see Krupskaya; I see Lenin's forehead or, rather, the top of his head.

The seamen entered on the left. I thought, "Kronshtadt sailors." They didn't have to be from Kronshtadt, but that's what I thought. They didn't wear their peacoats but came bare-chested. It must have started snowing outside, because snow dusted their tar-flap collars and shoulders, and their chest hairs were wet. They were big young men, really huge. They walked in a tight formation. The sergeant of the first squad stopped when he came up to Lenin, cried "Oy, mother!" and dropped to the floor. There was no confusion. The sailors picked up their sergeant and, their blue eyes filled with tears, walked past. I felt like they were leaving the sea for the last time, never to return. I then realized that they kept quietly lifting to their feet those in their ranks who had fainted. I see the back of Lenin's head or, rather, his high forehead. I hear the funeral march. The four columns of people flowing through no longer interest me. I look at Lenin and I want to cry. Anushka, I don't give a damn if you can or can't cry while standing guard, I want to cry—but can't.

I didn't ask Anushka, "What did you do that night?"

I have guests. They came from the faraway places in my life. Ahmet smiled. "What life have I had that it should have its nears and fars," he thought, "I've just lived a hand's-span." Today I didn't think even once about the possibility of being shot by Ismail's gun—well, *my* gun and bullets, but he'll pull the trigger. Dear Anushka, what are you doing now? What are you doing this second, the very second I asked what you're doing now? Suddenly I heard the engine. *Dum-dum-da-dum-dum.* I'd forgotten it. If you hear the same sound continuously, you keep hearing it but forget it. I was happy, as if I'd run into an old friend I hadn't seen in ages. I listened to it a long time. Then I forgot it again.

First Kerim's yellow eyes under his bushy black eyebrows, then all of him.

We're standing on the Bridge in Istanbul. It's overcast, just about to rain. He and I have come back from Moscow together. We were selling the first issue of our paper. We planned to stand in different places—I on the Bridge and he in Kasımpaşa, by the pools. But when we got to the Bridge, I asked, "Just stay with me for a few minutes, will you?"

"You scared?"

"Scared? Of what? No. I just don't know if I can shout, '*Hammer & Sickle!* Hot off the press!'"

"Are you embarrassed?"

"Something like that. I've never sold anything."

"And I have? My father was a street hawker?"

"Don't get mad. I just don't know how my voice will come out."

"You come from pashas, son—from pashas."

Kerim took a paper from the pile under his arm and, waving it around wildly, shouted: "Socialist newspaper! The latest news!"

People passing by don't even turn their heads. And it starts sprinkling.

I pull out a paper from the pile under my arm. Kerim shoves his paper in the faces of people hurrying by so as not to get caught in the rain: "Newspaper, new socialist paper!"

Nobody pays any attention. Even those who show some interest take one look at Kerim—who doesn't look much like a newsboy—and snap, "No thanks," and keep walking.

"God, doesn't one honest man cross this Bridge?"

"Newspaper! Damn it, won't we sell a single paper on this cursed Bridge? But you'll see, it'll be snapped up in Kasımpaşa."

My eye caught the headline of the paper in my hand: "Workers of the World, Unite!" As if somebody had suddenly stuck a knife in me, I started screaming at the top of my lungs, surprising myself with my own voice: "Workers of the world, unite! Workers of the world . . . Newspaper"—I scream for dear life!—"Unite! Newspaper, newspaper!"

"Okay, let's see how the world's workers will unite."

A well-dressed, graying gentleman wanted a paper. I almost hugged him in joy. I handed him the paper. "Here's your money, son." I noticed that he was handing me money only after he spoke. He laughed. "When I was young, in Paris," he said, "the socialists sold their papers this way."

That day, I sold 45 papers on the Bridge; Kerim sold 225 in Kasımpaşa.

. . .

We're slowly walking toward Red Square. Before us, behind us, people, flags, banners, pictures, songs. Our group is singing the May Day march: "1 May, 1 May, our one desire!" Anushka joins us. We've taught her the march, and she sings it in Turkish. I take her hand. Kerim says, "Are you afraid she'll run off somewhere?"

"I don't know. I'm always afraid I'll suddenly lose her—that out of the blue she'll turn into smoke or a bird and fly away somewhere."

"Are you serious? Or just kidding?"

"I'm serious."

"I thought people thought such things only in novels."

We slowed down, then came to a full stop. The Caucasians were behind us. They quickly cleared a circle, put a young man at the center, and started the Sheik Shamil dance. A young man from Daghestan, the handsomest guy at the university, starts dancing at the center. Anushka let my hand go and went to watch. And I followed. The man first bends down, as if praying; before Sheik Shamil fought the Tsarist armies, he used to pray, and this prayer ritual is danced at a very slow tempo, which suddenly changes: Sheik Shamil leaps up, pulls out his dagger, and, spinning on his toes, starts fighting. The young man is like a blond flash of lightning. But I've had enough of this dance. I respect, even love, Sheik Shamil, but whether Caucasian, Azeri, Armenian, Georgian, or Daghestani, under different names, with or without prayers—maybe there are other details, but they escape me—nobody misses the slightest opportunity to jump up and start this dance.

A couple of other young men and girls joined the dance. And people clapped, keeping time. I asked Anushka, "You like this dance that much?"

"Yes, I can't stop looking."

"At the Daghestani?"

"You're disgusting. But supposing at him. So what?"

We started moving again. Groups on side streets waited to join the march. "*Our* bakers!" Kerim exclaimed. On the side street, with their *zipkas*, caps, and flags both with and without the star and crescent, are our Black Sea men. "1 May" was written in Turkish on their banners. Russia had countless local cooperatives of Laz bakers, but their central cooperative is new. And the Chinese are in the business of laundry and ironing. But both our workers and the Chinese keep their own citizenship. They vote in the Soviet elections and can be elected, join the syndicates, or become members of the Bolshevik Party. Me, for example, a Turkish national, if I stand for election, I can be voted to the presidency of the Supreme Soviet. My God, how beautiful! So many parts of the world exist in one immense country! Here you're not asked your religion, country, or nationality. No. Instead, you're asked: "Do you live by exploiting others? Have you been a priest or a hodja? Have you worked for the police, the bourgeois gendarmes?" And if you answer, "No," you're okay, and you become a part of this great country, as if you were born here. What a beautiful thing, Anushka, how beautiful! To fall in step with people whose language you don't know, whose customs and traditions you don't know, and not feel like an alien. Feeling like an alien must be very sad, Anushka; I don't know, I've never lived through it, but an Albanian gardener who worked at my grandfather's seaside house had lived in Istanbul for who knows how many years. "Istanbul is beautiful," he'd say, "God bless its owners. But I'm afraid I'll die here, far from home."

Suddenly we heard a commotion, a disturbance in the ranks ahead of us. They were Japanese students. All hell broke loose in Japanese. Before we knew what was going on, the Japanese closed their ranks. Three militiamen carried something away. A man from Japanese political intelligence had recognized the Japanese students and was taking their pictures. Most of the kids had come to Moscow illegally. They swooped down on the wretch and tore his camera apart, along with him, too, I think. Or maybe they just beat him up and left him there. We asked

Petrosian, and he said, "Yes, they just roughed him up," but his eyes had a funny smile. We had stopped because of the incident. We started again, slowly making our way to Red Square. Men and women, Moscow's workers and clerks, under the flags and banners of their districts, factories, and associations, with their kids on their shoulders, moved along on both sides of us. In 1917, they had turned the White Moscow of the Tsars and merchants into the Red Moscow of today under the walls of the Kremlin and Krasnaya Presnya. I squeezed Anushka's hand.

Ahmet smiled sadly. He keeps remembering how tightly he held Anushka's hand whenever he could.

He realized it was long past his lunch hour. It was two o'clock. He's determined to eat hot food today. He'd been craving hot food for a long time: white beans with lots of red pepper.

Ismail was late again. He put the papers in his hand on Ahmet's clothes on the chair. He listened to the motor. "They've fixed the piston."

He started undressing. Ahmet mumbled in his sleep.

Ismail would first be arrested three years from this night, in 1928. Tried in Izmir and sent to Diyarbakır Prison, he'd spend two years there and be released. Arrested again in 1931, he'd be tried and sent to Bursa Prison. There, in 1932, Ismail would meet Neriman in the visiting room, on the opposite side of the wire screen. Neriman had come from Istanbul to visit her brother, Osman, a bank accountant in for embezzlement. Ismail was talking to his mother or, rather, shouting at her so she could hear him where she sat, next to the young girl. Both sides of the screen were packed, and everybody shouted. Osman Bey pointed out Neriman with his hand: "Meet my sister."

Neriman smiled, her dark eyes still with something of a child in them. Ismail waved. His mother: "The young lady and I came on the same boat from Istanbul. And she's been such a help to me in the hotel," she shouted. "God bless her."

Neriman smiled. Ismail shouted: "Thank you, Neriman Hanım."

"The young lady and I are at the same hotel. Our rooms are connected."

Ismail smiled at Neriman. Osman Bey shouted: "Next time, I'll get the director's permission to meet in the warden's room."

Until visiting hours ended, Neriman and Ismail eyed each other across the screen from the corners of their eyes.

Osman Bey and Ismail were in the same ward. Together they ate the pistachio lokum—Hadji Bekir's brand, yet (from Neriman); the sausage—Apikoğlu's (also from Neriman); and the stuffed eggplant (from Ismail's mother). That night, as Osman Bey wolfed down the eggplant dolmas, he suddenly spoke of Ahmet: "Ismail, Ahmet was a real gourmand" (Osman Bey is making this up on the spot, because he doesn't know that Ismail knows Ahmet). "Back in those days, Bolu didn't even have a beanery, let alone a restaurant, and Ahmet kept grumbling, 'And Bolu cooks are so famous in Istanbul.' I'll never forget one night, in a room on the second floor of the Mulers' Inn. After having convened our court as usual and sentenced a village agha to ten years, I brought out the grape-leaf dolmas I'd cooked that day with my own hands. Ahmet and Yusuf practically fell off their chairs in shock."

Now every time he hears Osman Bey tell stories of Bolu that he'd once heard from Ahmet in Izmir, Ismail feels a strange kind of sorrow he can't explain, not even to himself.

Six days later, they met in the warden's room. The room had an iron bed covered with a threadbare blanket, a writing table with a torn black-oilcloth cover mottled with purple ink stains, and three chairs. The *falaka* hung on the wall.

Neriman and Ismail's mother sat on the chairs, Osman Bey and Ismail on the bed. They had one hour. Osman Bey told stories that began like "When I was in Berlin, one night the Spartakists..." He asked Neriman how things were at school—she was a grade-school teacher in Istanbul. He praised Ismail to Ismail's mother: "I know these socialists from way back, and I was mixed up in it myself, but these are decent kids; you keep your heart strong, Hanım, and one day, one way or another . . . " and other words like that.

Neriman barely spoke. Her voice, a little guttural, didn't go with her eyes, which hadn't lost all their childhood. Ismail's mother enjoyed Osman Bey. Ismail and Neriman didn't exchange a single word.

Two months later, Neriman came down for the day again. Osman Bey asked Ismail to join him in the visiting room. Ismail and Neriman talked, shouting and screaming to each other. Neriman inquired about his mother. Ismail asked when final exams began. Osman Bey said an amnesty was certain on the tenth anniversary of the Republic.

"Then Ismail will be with us every day in Istanbul. That means you'll have another brother, Neriman."

Neriman asked: "Won't you go to your mother's in Manisa, Ismail Bey?"

"If we get out, of course I'll stop and see her. But I'll live in Istanbul."

That night, Ismail dreamed about Neriman. Women always fill the dreams of men in prison. Sometimes the most unthinkable women appear in your dreams, sometimes women you can barely stand to look at. Some have no hair or face. They don't all listen to the Devil and tempt you. You want them to tempt you, but these heathens refuse. And Neriman didn't listen to the Devil. She took Ismail's arm, and you know those giant steps in gymnastics? With steps like that, they flew through the ward, arm in arm, not touching the ground.

Ismail got out in the '33 amnesty, and he went to Manisa to see his mother. When he returned to Istanbul, between attending cell meetings, looking for work, printing posters, and nailing them up at night, he didn't have a free minute. Only on one Sunday afternoon could he go to Osman Bey's house in Kadıköy. Osman Bey wasn't home. On one of the side streets near Süreyya Cinema, in the first-floor parlor of an ugly, narrow stone house, he drank the coffee Neriman made for him. Inside the house it's silent. And the street has the desolation of early afternoons. A soft, warm breeze through the open window lightly swells the lace curtains. Neriman is wearing a short-sleeved dress. They don't talk. Ismail remembers how they flew through the ward. He looks at the girl's bare arms: gold hair, brown skin, plump. The Devil says, "Just touch those arms."

"Ismail Bey, you're quiet."

"I haven't much to say. You talk."

"How's your mother?"

"Fine, thank you. Is Osman's business doing well?"

"I suppose. I don't understand much, and I don't ask. Women should not meddle in men's business."

"What do you mean? You work like a man, bless you. You're earning your living."

"Yes, but still . . . A woman is a woman, even if she supports a house all by herself."

Ismail spoke of the equality of men and women. "Women must be liberated, working women, not only from capital but from the exploitation of the washboard, the kitchen," and words like that. As Neriman listened, her black eyes with something of childhood still in them sometimes looked amazed and sometimes pleased, but she never agreed with Ismail.

A month later, Ismail was arrested again. He did about eight months in Sultanahmet Prison, its stone cells with lone windows opening only to narrow halls cut off from other parts of the prison. It's the same on both floors. The Communists stay on the upper floor. It was visiting day. Ismail and Kerim talked about Ahmet. Kerim remembered how they'd sold papers on the Bridge in '25.

"Let that be, and tell me the truth about the girl in Moscow. You were sweet on her, but she couldn't get you to say, 'I love you very much'?"

Kerim scratched his bushy eyebrows. "I was a mortal enemy of lies at that time"—he took a drag on his cigarette—"and of cigarettes. I got used to cigarettes—to both."

Ismail: "Then give me a cigarette."

Kerim searched his pockets, took out three cigarettes, and handed one over. Ismail broke the cigarette in two and put one half in his long wooden cigarette holder.

"Ziya used to call bumming cigarettes the lowest form of panhandling."

"He was right."

Ismail started whistling through his teeth the "Tenth Year of the Republic" march. Then he took his cigarette holder out of his mouth: "You know, brother, the poets wrote this march about the soldiers: 'In ten years of war, we created fifteen million *ers*'—soldiers. Then they realized that the 'fifteen million *ers*'—when sung aloud—sounded like 'fifteen millionaires,' get it? And they changed the words to 'fifteen million fighters.'"

Kerim: "They messed it up," he said, and repeated: "In ten years of war we created fifteen millionaires of all ages."

"Our aghas lost their revolutionary zeal long ago, Ahmet used to say. Wait—he even put a number on how much they'd lost: eighty percent."

"Eighty or ninety percent, I don't know, but they drowned the Suphis, they did not solve the land problem, and they fear workers organizing like they fear wildfire. What's left to do? Sign a pact with imperialism?"

"And they will, brother, you'll see."

"What's left to do? A new alphabet, hats, civil law, separation of religion and the state . . ."

"They've started reading the Koran in the army."

"The hodjas were 'evil' when they supported the Caliphate, but now they sing the praises of the Republican Party. Sure, it serves their purposes."

The yard foreman shooed away the pigeons in the prison courtyard and shouted up to the cells: "Master Ismail! You've got a visitor, Master Ismail."

Everyone crossed Ismail's mind except Neriman.

"Neriman Hanım, what a surprise!"

"My brother couldn't come. He sends his regards. He had to go to Ankara on business."

"Give him my thanks. You proved more faithful than me. I could stop by your house only once. Really, sister, you'll never know how happy you've made me . . ." Damn it! (Ahmet saying "Damn it" all the time instantly flashed through his mind.) "Forgive me, Neriman Hanım, for this wretched habit of speech; I'm so used to saying 'brother.'"

The place wasn't really crammed with inmates and visitors. They could talk without being pushed and shoved and didn't have to shout at the top of their lungs. Suddenly Ismail said: "The police keep a record of who comes to see us."

"Let them. I'm not political."

That night, Ismail turned over to the commune the Hadji Bekir lokum Neriman had brought. The Communists in prison had set up a commune: food, drinks, cigarettes, and money given anyone would be placed in the middle, and food would be cooked in a common pot. That night, as he handed over the box of Hadji Bekir lokum to the commune, Ismail was as proud as if he had handed over something that would drive everybody crazy with joy.

The day after he got out of Sultanahmet Prison, Ismail crossed over to Kadıköy. Neriman was not home. He and Osman went to the sweets shop on Altıyol. Osman was in real estate.

"Osman Bey, maybe you're afraid to associate with me?"

"Why should I be afraid?" He paused in thought. "Look, I can't remember if it was in '25 or '24, in Tepebaşı, I think, I came face to face with Ahmet. I pretended not to know him and walked on. Back then, I was working for the Agriculture Bank, but I'm a free man now."

Neriman and Ismail first kissed on Kalamış Bay. Shimmering moonlight, the sea flat as a sheet. He rented a rowboat at the pier in Moda. A jazz band played in the nightclub at Kalamış, and people were dancing. The sea was full of rowboats. Ismail pulled on the oars. They sailed out toward Fenerbahçe. The Fenerbahçe lighthouse flickered on and off. The Islands' ferry sailed across the way, all glittering lights. "The ship with a hundred masts, where is the port it sails for?" Ismail put down the oars and went to sit with Neriman in the stern:

"Sister, may I kiss you just once?"

Neriman didn't answer.

"Are you saying this business doesn't require permission?"

He kissed Neriman. The boat lightly swayed to the waves kicked up by the Islands' ferry.

"The world's beautiful, sister!"

Neriman, with great seriousness, her guttural voice now really deep, repeated:

"The world's beautiful, brother."

Five months later, Ismail was back inside. He did ten months at the police headquarters. Neriman carried food to Ismail. They didn't let them see each other. "What's Ismail to you?" they asked.

"He's my fiancé," she said.

Ismail's trial, held while he was in custody, lasted a year and a half. Neriman kept coming to Sultanahmet Prison. She sat in the courtroom on the first day of the trial and on the day the verdict was read. She kept smiling at Ismail. She didn't attend the sessions in between; the hearings, as always, were closed to the public.

Ismail got out. He saw Neriman every Sunday. They kissed and hugged, but that's all.

Ismail tried to interest Neriman in politics and communism, but she couldn't care less. Only when he told her about the lives of the revolutionaries—what he'd heard from those who'd been in Moscow, and what he'd read with the little Russian he'd learned (in prison Ismail studied both Marxism and Russian.)—would she listen excitedly. Especially the lives of the women of the revolution, Krupskaya's especially.

"A faithful, loyal woman, she gave her whole life to her man."

"That's not the point, sister; she gave her whole life to the revolution."

"Yes, yes, Ismail, but how devoted she was to Lenin! At once his wife, his mother, and certainly his friend, too—but just look at the love in that woman."

Ismail couldn't find a steady job. What with running from his persecutors, he had no time to chase down jobs. He earned his pocket money working at small foundries, repair shops, and the like. He got into a factory once, but the police had him fired after a week.

"Neriman, would you want to be on that freighter sailing by?"

They sit under a pistachio tree on the hill in Emirgan. Stretched out below them, the Bosporus meanders, widening and narrowing. A black freighter with a single smokestack, half its propeller above water whipping it up to a froth, headed for the Black Sea.

"No. What would I do on that freighter? Where's it headed?"

"Who knows, maybe Odessa. You wouldn't even want to go to Odessa?"

"I would, with you. But the place I like best in the whole world is right here under this pistachio tree."

"What if a genie jumped out of a bottle now and said, 'Tell me your wish, Neriman—anything.'"

"What would I wish for? Wait, let me think. I wouldn't want much. I have one or two things I want in this life. First, I'd wish Ismail didn't go to prison again, never ever. That's the first. Then I would wish we had a house—with a yard, of course, somewhere here on Emirgan hill, of course, a pretty little house full of people. I wouldn't want money or anything, absolutely not. And health, of course. But you're—knock on wood—strong as a lion, and my health isn't bad."

"You're fit as a fiddle."

"That would be all."

"Totally petit-bourgeois."

"You've labeled me that several times now, Ismail. If that's what I am, that's what I am."

"Don't get mad."

"I'm not."

"But don't you care at all about the people outside your garden walls, people stricken with hunger or wasted from working like dogs?"

"Why wouldn't I care? If I could have wishes for others, I would ask the Arabian genie to give everyone a little house with green shutters wherever they wanted, and wish no one went hungry. And no one had to work the way you said."

"There are no Arabian genies. We are the Arabs. We, the working classes of the world, we will bring about a free world—without classes or borders, a world where all men will be brothers."

"You're the one who brought up the Arab, but you're mad at me."

"I'm not mad. It's class warfare, that's all, sister. And I'll go to prison if necessary."

"And you, you're obliged to go inside every so often to bring about this new world!"

Ismail didn't respond. He hummed his favorite march:

> Comrades in prisons,
> inside four stone walls,
> no longer in our ranks;

> when the red day dawns, have your gun at the ready
> and fight for the proletariat's cause,
> your cause, the proletarians' fight.

Ismail lit a cigarette. Ahmet was still grumbling something in his sleep. Ismail listened to what he was saying, but couldn't make it out. Ismail picked up the Istanbul paper; the year was 1925. He read the news item on the second page one more time. He put down the paper, blew out the lamp, and went to sleep.

In the winter of '38, they arrested Ismail again. They sent him to Ankara, where they threw him in solitary in the military prison. Solitary is a stone cell. The window has iron bars but no glass. Snow blows inside. And the floor is cement. Forget a mattress—the bastards didn't even give me a blanket. As Ismail paced up and down, he went back thirteen years to the cottage in Izmir and remembered how the bristly blanket had pricked his chin, how Ahmet kept blowing at the light but couldn't blow it out.

Ismail could see Neriman only after he was sentenced in Ankara and sent to prison in Istanbul, to the Mehterhane.

"They won't keep me here. They're going to exile me somewhere. We'll see where."

Neriman could hardly hold back her tears. Then, trying to smile, she said, "I spoke to a lawyer. We can get married even when you're in prison. Let's have a marriage ceremony, brother. If I'm your wife, it'll be easier for me to come and see you. Wherever they exile you, I'll move there. Maybe they won't let me teach, but I can take in sewing, and we'll manage."

A month later, early one morning two naval sergeants, a naval officer, and three privates slapped handcuffs on his wrists and marched him out of the Mehterhane, without a word about what was happening or where they were taking him. They put him on a navy boat, at the Kadıköy Pier under the Bridge, and took him to the *Erkin*, the supply ship for the submarine fleet anchored off the Islands. On the way, Ismail tried to figure out by himself what was going on. He suddenly thought of Sergeant Ferhat. But nothing had happened between them beyond exchanging casual greetings. A couple of times they'd shared a table at the same bar. That was all.

They threw Ismail in the crew's latrine on the *Erkin*. They'd closed the portholes. The floor was covered with urine a hand's-span deep, and shit floated in the urine. The stench, the stench and the heat. For a while Ismail just stood there. He whistled. His eye caught the closed porthole of the door. He saw an officer's head. The head pulled back, and another officer's head appeared. "The bastards are watching to see what I'm going to do." He sat down in the pool of urine. He lit a cigarette. And started singing. But the question remained in his head: *Why did they take me here?*

They removed Ismail from the latrine late that afternoon. Flanked by a sergeant and two privates with bayonets, he descended many steps—narrow, winding iron stairs. They opened an iron door and shoved Ismail into the darkness. They shut the door. He felt around with his hands—things like spools or barrels. The storage bilge. He took off his shirt. He took off his pants. He was in his underwear. But he couldn't stop sweating. He sat on a coil of ropes, his eyes adjusting to the dark. He slept.

"Get up. Get dressed."

Dazzled by the spotlight in his eyes, he turned his head away.

"Get up. Get dressed."

The spotlight probed the bilge, scanning the coils of rope and spools, barrels, iron chains. Ismail saw the officer in his white uniform standing at the door, holding the spotlight. Behind the officer, a wilderness of pipes in a narrow, lead-gray iron corridor, and two privates with bayonets standing under the yellow light of the glass bulbs. He couldn't tell if it was day or night—the light bulbs had been on when they took him down here. He got dressed.

"March."

Ismail in front, the officer and the privates following, they climbed a narrow iron staircase. The ship shook with the roar of its working engines. "We must be moving," Ismail thought.

"Turn left."

They stood on a narrow landing, with cages of metal grating and pipes thin and thick, and masses of electric cables right and left, over and under. Ismail turned to the staircase on the left and started climbing. "They're taking me up for questioning. But why? What will they ask me? What am I doing here with these men?"

They stepped out on deck, into the cool night.

"Keep going. Don't look back."

There's nothing ahead of Ismail but the starry night. The deck is deserted. The roar of the engines beat the shushing sea—open sea without end, its waves' white crests visible in the dark. The warship slowly plunged ahead. Ismail thought: "No one knows I'm here . . . But they must have signed some papers or something when they took me out of the Mehterhane. But where are we going? Am I afraid? Not yet . . ."

"Walk and don't look back."

There wasn't much space left to walk. The railing was two steps away.

"Halt."

He stopped. He heard behind him the clicks of guns cocking. He suddenly thought of Mustafa Suphi. "So they'll shoot me and dump me overboard. But why? If these goons decided to take me out, there are easier ways, but why, why are they so determined?" All this went through his head, not clearly like this but all in a blur. "I should turn around and jump them."

He didn't think this clearly, either, but something like this went through his head. He turned around. He saw the barrels of the two bayonet rifles aimed at him and the white uniform of the officer. At that instant another officer appeared next to the first. He whispered something to him. The first officer told Ismail: "Turn around, walk."

They descended the same steps. Ismail stepped into the dark of the bilge. Took off his clothes. Stretched out on the ropes. "They faked something. But why take me here?"

Ismail had a dream that night. He and Neriman were on a galleon, at the stern. A galleon in full sail. So many sails, all full-blown, as if the ship's about to fly. The helm is not a helm but a huge water-wheel. Barbaros Hayrettin turns the wheel, his beard flaming-red. Neriman asks Barbaros: "Why is your beard so red?"

"Instead of worrying about my beard, look at your husband's beard."

Ismail has a bright green beard down to his navel. He and Neriman lie on their backs on uncut green grass somewhere above the Bosporus; Ismail can't quite tell where. They're watching fluffy white clouds. Ismail puts out his hand and touches Neriman's breast as if by accident.

"What are you doing?" says Neriman.

"Am I not your husband?"

"We're not married yet."

"Why aren't we married?"

"My bridal gown isn't ready yet, that's why."

"So when will it be ready?"

"Tomorrow."

Barbaros: "We're sailing to Odessa, if the wind doesn't fail."

Neriman: "I don't want to go to Odessa."

Ismail: "I'll introduce you to Krupskaya."

"Isn't Krupskaya dead?"

"Why would she be dead?"

But he realizes he doesn't know if Krupskaya is dead or alive.

Osman Bey and Ahmet and also Yusuf. Ismail can't make out Yusuf's face. They're in the room above the Mulers' Inn. They've set up court among the mules standing there, shaking the bells and tassels around their necks. Ahmet says to Ismail: "You be the judge tonight instead of me."

Ismail asks for five years for the officer in the white uniform who aimed the spotlight at his eyes. Neriman: "You're merciless."

"What is mercy?" Ismail screams. Neriman is crying. Ismail hugs her. They kiss.

The white-uniformed officer with the spotlight shouts: "Enough! Fire!"

The bullets enter Ismail's back, exit in the front, and fall at his feet, scattering on the deck. Ismail jolted awake.

For two nights, they walked Ismail around the deck of the *Erkin*. Then they brought him before the military prosecutor. In a search conducted by the navy, the books of a Communist poet were found in the lockers of privates and sergeants. These were all books sold legally in stores. One of the books was found in Sergeant Ferhat's locker. Ferhat told them, "It's not my book. Somebody must have put it in my locker." They pressed him. He said, "I know a Communist named Ismail." Ismail gathered all this from the prosecutor's indictment. He didn't have any deposition to give the prosecutor, who didn't seem much interested in Ismail's statement. He was a dark little man obsessed with radios. Especially with repairing them. He knew that Ismail understood radios—from the police reports he learned that, at the time of Ismail's last arrest, he had been working in a radio repair shop—and they talked mostly about radios. Their shared interest in this subject created something like a bond between them. He ordered Ismail removed from the bilge and lodged in a sergeant's cabin. Once, Ismail said: "Şerif Bey, when I was first here, why did they take me out on deck at midnight? They made like they would shoot me in the back and throw me overboard."

"The naval chief of staff read somewhere, in a German book, about psychological torture. But you didn't fall for it. When I came here and learned about it, I told them, 'Give it up. We don't need that torture.'"

The trial was held in the big hall on board ship. The day the sentences were read, three rows of chairs were placed between the judges and the prisoners, probably to keep the prisoners from attacking the judges. Ismail saw Şerif Bey for the last time a week before the hearings began. They talked about radio repair again. Then Şerif Bey, picking at his gleaming white teeth with a pencil, said, "Ismail, we're both, in our own fields, hardened men. You've noticed how many times I asked if you'd formed a cell with Ferhat. And I was convinced long ago that you hadn't. But that's not the point. We're entering the war on the German side. We'll take Mosul from the British, Batum from the Russians, and Aleppo from the French. Do you understand? We need a good housecleaning, and we're starting with you people and finishing up with the British. Who knows, one day you might meet Ismet Pasha inside." (Ismail did not meet Ismet Pasha inside, and Turkey did not enter the war or side with Germany. The naval chief of staff, openly sympathetic to the Germans, was forced to retire under pressure from Britain; nothing happened to Şerif Bey).

They tacked a second sentence on to Ismail's original sentence. They also convicted five sergeants and three privates. It came out in the hearings that Sergeant Major Ali planted the book in Ferhat's locker there; the two had fought over a woman. But to free Ferhat would mean they'd also have to let Ismail go. And freeing Ismail would leave "the Communist plot in the navy" without a leader.

Ismail was exiled to a prison in central Anatolia. By himself. High walls enclosed the prison, said to have been left over from the Genoese. In many places in central Anatolia, all old buildings, all the remains of old monuments, are said to be left over from the Genoese. The walls were huge blocks of stones just piled one on top of another, without mortar or anything. And they were very wide—two armed guardsmen paced on them. On the first floor of the prison, small shops were rented out to prisoners: a tailor, a tinsmith, two carpenters, four cobblers, and a mirror-maker. The cells were on the second floor, side by side and set back behind a projection spanning the length of the building like a balcony but without a railing

The first floor housed the administration, the head guard's room, two solitary cells, and a dungeon. In the yard stood a fountain and a stunted little tree. Who knows what kind of tree? They put Ismail in the third ward. A month later Neriman came: "I'll find a teaching job here," she said, "I'm very hopeful." They put off the marriage till after Neriman's transfer. "It's strategy, sister. Not that anybody will fall for it, but you never know. If the Ministry knew you were my wife, they might not transfer you here." Neriman left. Ismail didn't think, "I've tied her up for many years, how many more years will she wait for me? Let her go and take her chances somewhere else." On the contrary, before Neriman was transferred and returned, he learned from the prison director how they could get married. When Neriman came back, and after the banns were posted, a lawyer was hired to act as Justice of the Peace, and the marriage was performed in the Marriage Bureau of City Hall. They walked up dimly lit, rickety wooden stairs. Neriman wore a gray suit. They unlocked Ismail's handcuffs before the acting Justice of the Peace, who wished them, in a tired but very sincere voice, "A long, happy life." He congratulated them. The witnesses were the head guard and the seargant-at-arms of City Hall.

The next day was visiting day. The director gave permission for them to meet, just this once, in his room, but he never left his desk. Pretending to be busy with the paperwork before him, he eyed Neriman and Ismail. They sat side by side on a threadbare velvet couch with broken springs. They didn't say a word. The director said two or three times: "Don't be embarrassed; you can talk. There's nothing to be embarrassed about. Don't mind me, I'm so swamped with work, I wouldn't hear a cannon go off. Say something, you're newlyweds."

Each time, Ismail answered, "Thank you, we'll talk." But they didn't. Once, Ismail reached for Neriman's hand, but she pulled it back and glared at Ismail as if he should be ashamed.

Ismail woke up to Ahmet screaming as if he was being strangled. He walked over in the dark and nudged him.

"Huh?" Ahmet said and woke up.

Ismail lit the lamp: "You were screaming in your sleep again."

"Can I have a glass of water?"

He gulped down the water as if he had been parched for days. "I'm sorry!"

"Want a cigarette?"

"No. I think I have a fever."

Ismail felt Ahmet's forehead: "You don't."

"Are those today's papers?"

"You can read them tomorrow."

Ahmet reached over and took the papers.

"I have to busy myself with something now to take my mind off it."

He glanced at the Izmir paper and put it down. He picked up the Istanbul paper, and on the second page he stopped. "They arrested Kerim."

"Yes."

"The bastards. It doesn't say how they caught him. The bastards. God damn it."

THE TWENTY-THIRD LINE

WHEN HE WOKE UP the next morning, the first thing Ahmet thought about was Kerim's arrest. He read the news once again. He got up. Ismail had left the lamp on. Damn that motor sound! Still in his underwear, he walked over to the food cupboard. I obviously have a fever. He put his hand in his armpit. I have a fever. He sat on the chair, on his clothes. And I ache all over. He started to make tea but changed his mind. And I'm nauseous. He leaned against the rough stones of the wall. So it's started. He lay on his back. Did the book say anything about running a fever? It talked about aching muscles, and I think nausea, too. It talked about headaches—like being squeezed in a vise. The book didn't say anything about a vise. My head aches. I didn't realize it till just now, but I have a terrible headache. And I have a fever. But the book, about running a fever... The book lay on the table, its corner sticking out under the newspapers. I won't look. What's the difference if it says a high fever? Everything else is in order—the muscle pain, the headache, the nausea. I won't look; while I croak, let's at least have this much will power. He's sinking, as if into a warm bath after a long, hard journey, deeper into sorrow. Suddenly he sat up. He dressed as if fighting with someone. He made tea. First, he forced himself to drink, then enjoyed the tea. He was sweating. And there's no thermometer... Maybe it was around somewhere—left over from Ziya. He walked, unsteady, and looked around. He couldn't find it. He checked himself. The nausea was almost gone. He had forgotten about the book. He lay down. His head was growing bigger and bigger; it couldn't fit within the four walls of the cottage, but wasn't heavy—it was like a huge head of foam.

"Petrosian, Anushka says she could fall in love with you."

"And she'd do well if she did."

"And you with her?"

"And I with her. But we're too late. A Turkish boy came between us."

"Say the word, and I'll get out."

"It's no use now, even if you get out. Us Armenians, is there anything we haven't suffered at the hands of you Turks? You made mincemeat of us."

"I wasn't there when they massacred you."

"And you're not alone . . . If you really look at it, even the Turkish peasants who were handed the knives weren't there; that's the truth. They were handed the weapons, made into armed men, and pushed to slaughter."

"But still, they dishonored my people."

Si-Ya-U: "What nation doesn't have a black mark against it? Didn't the British people slaughter us in Shanghai and starve the Indians to death?"

Anushka: "Well, then, the people should start getting their act together. The man who killed my father was a Russian, but he was an officer in the Kolchak army, a Pomeshchik. He knew why he killed my father. But the Kazakh horsemen? The Kazakh soldiers who slaughtered peasants, peasants just like themselves, should we forgive them, too, because they're common people?"

I: "Nobody's saying that."

Si-Ya-U: "Read Lenin's 'National Pride,' Anushka."

Anushka: "Look, I read it before you did. He also says he's ashamed when they put Russian peasants in uniform and send them off to crush other people."

Petrosian spoke in a tired voice: "Why are you arguing? You're all saying the same thing."

Anushka: "Not quite."

Petrosian asked out of the blue: "Anushka, do you ever think of dying?"

"I've seen it. And not just once."

"Who hasn't seen it? I didn't mean seeing others die or thinking about death in general. I asked whether you ever think of your *own* death. Did any of you here ever seriously think about it?"

We were all taken aback by Petrosian's question. If anyone had said he'd ask such a question, we wouldn't have believed it.

Si-Ya-U: "I haven't thought about it. I know I'm going to die, of course . . . I don't mean to say, 'There's nothing I can do about it, so why think about it?' I just haven't thought about it."

Anushka: "I have. When my mother was dying of typhus, I thought about it at her deathbed; it was just the two of us in the hovel. Plus death. It could have caught me, too, and carried me off. That's what I thought: it'll carry me off and never bring me back. Where will it take me? Nowhere. I haven't been a believer since fifteen. So I tried to think about this nowhere."

Petrosian couldn't hide his keen interest: "Could you ever visualize that nowhere?"

"No. And you? Forgive me . . . I meant . . . I . . ."

"Forgive you for what? I think about death. What would be more natural for me? You'd have to be stupid not to think about something that might happen very soon and change everything for you—at the very root." He was quiet. Then: "At tomorrow's party, Anushka, you must dance at least five dances with me."

We discussed this and that for another hour. We discussed Meyerhold. I suggested the Bolshoi would make a good wheat granary. Anushka got angry. I said the "Little Theater" was a museum. Anushka was about to claw my face. Petrosian joined our argument, roaring with laughter, siding now with Anushka and now with me. He got up. We saw him to the top of the stairs. As always, he climbed on the railing, waved at us, and slid down it from the fourth floor. Anushka screamed. We ran down, four steps at a time. Down there, on the stone floor, just beyond the first step, lay Petrosian, his head smashed.

One night, days later, Anushka, Si-Ya-U, and I were walking back from the Meyerhold after seeing *The Forest*—Si-Ya-U accompanied us everywhere now, to the movies, the theater—and I said: "Petrosian killed himself."

Anushka screamed as if I had personally insulted her: "No!"—she repeated with hatred—"No! You're lying!"

I said nothing. She took Si-Ya-U's arm. They stepped in front of me. We walked like that for a while. We were on the boulevard, walking toward the statue of Timiryazev—at the time, one of my favorite monuments in Moscow. Anushka dropped Si-Ya-U's arm and came up to me, her voice tearful: "Why did you say that? There's a sadistic side of you that's against me. You get pleasure from battering the best things that live in me."

I didn't understand what Anushka meant. I said nothing. I pulled her to me and kissed her. Si-Ya-U stood at a distance, his head down as if he were looking for something in the dark.

I'm not so sure Petrosian killed himself.

I thought all this when I had a huge head of foam. Not in this order, but it all ran through my head. Why these things and not others? I don't know.

Ahmet got up and swallowed three aspirins all at once. He drew the twenty-third line behind the door and threw himself on the bed.

When Ismail came home, he found Ahmet passed out but still dressed. In a sweat. He checked his wrist. He has a fever. And his heart is racing. The corner of the book sticking out from under the newspapers caught his eye. He opened it and read. He closed it. Ahmet: "Is that you, Ismail?"

"Let me help you get undressed."

"I'm not rabid, Ismail."

"Of course you're not."

"Read the book. Does it say anything about fever?"

"Why bother?"

"I say look it up."

Ismail couldn't say he'd already looked. He was ashamed. He opened the book and pretended to read.

"What does it say?"

"It doesn't say anything about a fever."

"Are you telling the truth?"

"Why would I lie, brother?"

"You're not Kerim; you can lie all right."

Ahmet fell back to sleep.

The day after they got married, sitting on the threadbare velvet couch with broken springs in the prison director's room, Ismail had wanted to hold Neriman's hand, and she'd looked at him as if he should be ashamed of himself. Ismail took back his hand. Neriman: "I got a letter from my brother. His sciatica is acting up again."

The director: "I've got sciatica, too. What does your brother take for it? Shots, salicylates, nothing helps. I even immersed myself up to my neck in hot springs—no relief."

"My brother takes pills."

"Pills are child's play. How old is your brother?"

"Oh, it's got nothing to do with age, but it's harder to treat in older people."

Ismail thought: "Older people?"

He suddenly realized he'd reached forty himself. How old was Neriman? She must be twenty-eight or twenty-nine. He gave Neriman a sidelong glance: she looks about twenty-two. And I'm forty. Life went past just like that. There's a book called *A Life Went Past like That*. Was it a bad life? Why should it be bad, brother? But it went by.

The director looked at his watch. Neriman: "I've got to go." She shook hands with Ismail and asked: "What should I take you next week?"

Ismail didn't respond. He's looking at Neriman's feet, noticing for the first time how small and shapely they are. And I'm forty.

One day Neriman appeared in the visiting room with a girl with a shaved head. Dressed like an Istanbul girl, about five or six. Ismail was most curious about the shaved head of the girl clutching Neriman's hand and looking around in fear: "Why did they shave her poor head?"

"Head lice. Not like you could treat with soap and medication. So I had her head shaved. Her hair will grow back thicker."

"*You* had her head shaved?"

"I adopted Emine. You and I have a daughter now."

Ismail laughed: "So Emine is our daughter? I just hope her hair grows back quick. But, sister, she's too skinny."

"In two months, she'll be nice and plump. And her hair will grow out. I think blue ribbons will look good on Emine. My Emine, I . . ."

Ismail understood: "You really want a child, Neriman?"

"Very much. And now I have one."

"So you want to be a mother?"

"Why wouldn't I? To be a mother . . . If you only knew, sometimes . . . But now I *am* a mother. And you're a father."

"Let's get divorced, Neriman."

"We got married only three months ago."

"Let's divorce after six months. You're a young woman— twenty-eight, twenty-nine. I'm a forty-year-old man. And who knows when I'll get out? I've ruined your life. You should get married and be a real mother."

Neriman started to cry, first silently, then sobbing aloud. Emine joined in. Of the people in the visiting room, neither the prisoners nor the visitors paid any attention. People sighing and crying on the visitors' side of the wire screen were common scenes. Ismail: "Stop it, sister. For God's sake, don't cry. I was just joking. And look at Emine: wipe the snot from her nose."

Neriman, trying to hold back her tears, dried Emine's nose with her handkerchief.

• • •

That night, Ismail sat in the window of his cell, clutching the iron bars with both hands. He gazed at the mountains across. The mountains are bare, but with a red glow. Over a hill the size of a handkerchief, as small as the one Neriman used to wipe Emine's nose, a little cloud hangs motionless in the darkening blue. Neriman is twenty-eight or twenty-nine, but she looks twenty-two, at most twenty-four. And she's healthy. I've never known her to be sick. Plus, what does this business have to do with health? A woman wants to be a mother. And here a girl, too, wants to be a mother. And a woman also wants a man. But a girl who hasn't known a man. . . . Oh, these are just words, brother—stuff we men make up. Why didn't I sleep with Neriman? Why didn't we get married while I was outside? Did we have to be married to sleep together? Would Neriman have given herself to me any other way? One day in the house in Kadıköy, it almost happened. Why didn't it? Because I'm an ass. The way Ahmet didn't touch Anushka. Lies. Before six months were out, they were cooking all right. Okay, but why did we get married now? I'm not the one who said, "Oh, we've got to get married." I didn't trick her. Oh, God damn it! Ahmet used to keep "Oh" out of it—"God damn it" without an "Oh." Me, Neriman . . . You, me, is that the matter? Is anyone accusing you?

The next morning, as he was getting a shave—he shaved only on visiting days, but this morning he made an exception—he asked the barber, Ali, who was in for murder: "How old do I look, Ali?"

"Forty, forty-five."

Ismail went to the tailor Ramiz's shop—he'd rented half of it and worked fixing radios and sewing machines. He worked glumly till nightfall.

Now and then Ismail's mother came up from Manisa and stayed a week or two with her daughter-in-law. Ismail begged her: "Come settle here, mother."

She wouldn't. "You can't have two households together. I love Neriman like my own daughter, but if we lived under the same roof, before six months were out we'd be at each other's throat. And I can't afford to keep a separate house here."

Most of the prisoners are peasants. The administration supplies seven-hundred grams of black bread. And water. And lights through the night. No beds, blankets, or clothing. Either your visitors deliver you things, or you find some way of managing inside.

One of the guards is from Bursa. He's very pro-German. Every night, after he says "God bless" and shoots the iron bolt from the outside, he puts his face up to the peephole and calls to Ismail: "Come over here, Master Ismail. Hitler torched London again. The Germans will win the war. Why be stubborn? Why not just admit it?"

And Ismail says: "They won't win."

And the guard: "Okay, have it your way."

And the next night they repeat the same conversation. This is the guard from Bursa at whose feet Ismail's mother collapsed and died. In the visiting room. Behind the wire screen.

"I brought you grape-leaf dolmas, Ismail. They got a little squished between Manisa and here. Share them with the guard effendi, too," she said. And she collapsed at the guard's feet.

Neriman was at home, sick with the flu—her first illness—so the poor woman had come alone. They took her to the county hospital. Heart failure, the doctors said. For six months now she's lain in the cemetery visible over the prison walls left by the Genoese. Ismail again sits in his windowsill, gazing at the cemetery that looks like a burnt-out field in the moonlight. He couldn't get used to his mother's death, because it was so hard for him to believe it. He saw her collapse before his eyes, and he saw, from this window, how she was carried to the cemetery early one afternoon, in harsh sunlight. But seeing, knowing, and being certain in this matter is one thing, and believing is another. About a month after her death, Neriman said: "I'm your mother now."

Ismail heard about Hitler's invasion of Russia in the shop while he was repairing the chief prosecutor's radio, a Phillips. He must have looked funny, because the tailor Ramiz asked: "What happened? What's wrong?"

"The dog thirsts for his death . . ."

"Who?"

Soon the whole prison had heard the news. "There'll be an amnesty—we'll get out," they said.

Ismail takes more and more time with his repairs, trying to follow the Soviet radio broadcasts with his rudimentary knowledge of Russian. Aside from a couple of newspapers like *Tan*, the press and Radio Ankara support the Germans. The guard from Bursa no longer taunts Ismail nightly with "Give it up, the Germans will win." Because Ismail lit into the guy and started cursing him from his mother on down. The guard didn't dare pull him behind the door and beat him up. After all, Ismail repaired even the governor's radio. But he became Ismail's sworn enemy. On visiting days, if he was on duty, he would go up to Neriman by the wire and poke around in the food she had brought with his iron stick until it became inedible.

Ismail was surprised when the Red Army retreated. He knew there wasn't a stronger army in the world. He had heard from people who had been to Moscow about the parades in Red Square and the parachutes raining from the sky. Why don't they rain down behind the German lines? he kept asking himself. Then he tried to convince himself that the retreat was deliberate, strategic. He couldn't believe hundreds of thousands of Red Army soldiers were taken prisoner. He started thinking that, even if the number was half of what Radio Berlin reported—or he *tried* to think, but his pain was so fierce he forced himself not to think.

• • •

The Germans closed in on Moscow. In *Cumhuriyet*, Abidin Daver wrote stuff like "It is a matter of days before Moscow falls."

Ismail paces the railless balcony of the wards. Over the Genoese walls, he can see the snowy mountains and roofs covered with snow across the way. The prison yard is also covered with snow. On his break, Ismail picked up a handful of slushy snow. He started eating it, trying to imagine Moscow. With what he had heard from Ahmet and others and from the few photographs he'd seen—he could draw by heart a picture of Lenin's tomb—he tried to imagine Moscow, snowy Moscow surrounded by Fascists. There, people are fighting for their lives while, here, we take it easy. I'm in agony, brother!

One day Neriman visited without Emine. "The school let me go."
"Why?"
"Orders of the Ministry."
"Why?"
"Don't worry, I'll take in sewing. It's better. I have my sewing machine. One part doesn't work right, but you can fix it."
"Sister, why did they fire you?"
"About a month ago—no, a month and a half—the geography teacher, a no-good hound dog, I never told you, but he was always harassing me."
"Harassing how? What do you mean?"
"Oh, nothing. Trashy talk. And he has a wife, too—for shame. Lots of times I put him in his place. The baldy."
Ismail felt stabbed in the back. He's bald, and he still bothers her. The town is full of men who aren't bald. A beautiful young woman. What's more, she's from Istanbul. And on top of it all, her husband is in jail—just reach out and pluck the fruit off the branch.
Neriman continued: "We were talking in the teachers' lounge, the headmaster . . ."

"He's after you, too?"

"N-o-o-o . . . You think everybody is assaulting me?"

"Why wouldn't they? You're a honey of a woman."

"Have you lost your mind? What do you think I am?"

"Okay, okay, so the headmaster?"

"He said it's good the Germans are butchering those Russians. Communists have no respect for family: your wife is mine, my wife is yours. The geography teacher turned to me: 'Neriman Hanım, your husband is a Communist. Does he believe that, too?' I lost it—I slapped the bastard."

"You did good. You did very good. Very good. Bravo, sister. But why didn't you tell me this before?"

"I didn't want you to worry."

"Did they fire you because you smacked the pig?"

"No. They said I made Communist propaganda. The headmaster and the geography teacher filed a report with the Ministry: 'Her husband is in prison, convicted of Communism,' they wrote. The other teachers all protested this injustice. They said, 'We'll sign a petition and demand your rights.' But I wouldn't go back to the school for anything. I'm going to take in sewing. And you'll see, I'll make more money."

Thirty men sleep in Ismail's ward. The floor is cement. A very wide, high, wooden platform runs along the walls, starting at one side of the door and ending at the other. The center is clear. In the right corner, at the head of the ward, stand Süleyman Agha's mattresses. When these mattresses, blankets, and pillows are piled on top of one another during the day, Süleyman Agha squats cross-legged on his prayer rug at the top and fingers his prayer beads all day long, sipping tea and coffee from the gas burner he operates in the ward. He's the agha of a big village two hours from town. He's in for ordering a hit. He had his shepherd shoot the agha of a neighboring village. They hanged the shepherd; they gave the agha fifteen years.

The tailor Ramiz is in the same ward, along with the tinsmith Şefik. The poor men's beds are worn-down to flattened thin mats. Most don't fold them up for the day but sit on them. The ward foreman sleeps by the door on a white lambskin fleece black with dirt. Süleyman Agha has his own private foreman. "Gay" Ihsan, they call him. He's poor. A young man with a paper-white face. They say Süleyman Agha uses Gay Ihsan like a woman.

Ismail's bed is next to the tailor Ramiz's.

Shoes, scarves, and rawhide moccasins are removed and left at the center of the ward. Gas burners, braziers, and Primuses—the noisiest is Süleyman Agha's, and the noisier the Primus, the more prestigious—burn at the center. In winter, people warm themselves by placing their burners and braziers between their legs. The stench of charcoal and gas fumes sometimes makes you feel like you'll pass out.

Süleyman Agha controls the hashish traffic inside. He also runs the gambling racket and takes his cut.

In 1942, the prisoners kicked out of Sivas Prison arrived: three heroin smugglers from Istanbul and two murderers from Izmir, their fame widespread through many prisons. And the "Adams" from Istanbul also arrived. The "Adams"—so called because they were destitute wretches—were assigned to the last ward, with the poorest peasants. They slept on newspapers spread out on their platforms. The others settled in the second ward on the right. And an artillery lieutenant caught spying for the Germans also arrived. They put him in Süleyman Agha's ward. Heroin traffic soon began inside, the market controlled by prisoners from Sinop. Before long, trouble started between the men from Sinop and Süleyman Agha: the Sinop men wanted to take over both his hashish trade and his gambling racket. The director sided with the Sinop men, the head guard with Süleyman Agha. The German-spy lieutenant first sided with Süleyman Agha, then switched sides and supported the Sinop men. The sergeant-major guardsman stood with the lieutenant. The Sinop men bought off Süleyman Agha's foreman, Gay Ihsan, and one day, when the agha was at his noon prayers, three of them burst into the ward and stabbed him in the back. Ismail and the tailor Ramiz were in the shop. The tinsmith Şefik was in the ward, warming up his lunch. He hollered down: "They've killed the agha! Help!"

The Sinop men knifed him, too. The guardsmen lined up on the Genoese wall. The sergeant-major whistled nonstop, screaming: "Nobody move—I'll give orders to shoot."

The Sinop men stayed downstairs in the dungeon for a month. Then they moved upstairs and settled in Süleyman Agha's ward. One day in the shop, the tailor Ramiz told Ismail: "I don't like that German lieutenant. He's talking trash about you. Watch out."

"What'll the thug do to me, brother? I have no business with hash or gambling."

"You know best, but still, watch out."

One Sunday two months later, Ismail returned from the visiting room and stepped into the prison gateway. Three Sinop men were waiting before the door, on their way to court for the Süleyman Agha incident. They were handcuffed. Suddenly, Gay Ihsan, the two other Sinop men, and the lieutenant appeared and attacked their friends, stabbing them in the back. Ismail yelled: "Stop it!"

The gatekeeper from Bursa blew his whistle. One of the handcuffed men, Murtaza from Izmir, managed to wrest the knife from Gay Ihsan and stuck him with it. The lieutenant saw this and lunged at Ismail. Ismail jumped back and beaned the guy with the heavy pot of food Neriman had just delivered.

An hour later Gay Ihsan, on his deathbed in the infirmary, his head resting on Ismail's lap, said: "Give me a glass of water, effendi."

Ismail gently put his head down on the torn white oilcloth of the examination table and gave him the water.

"It was my fate to take my last drop of water from your hands. And I was going to kill you, too. Forgive me."

"I forgive you."

Things got clearer by nightfall. The tailor Ramiz, stroking his light brown mustache, told Ismail: "Didn't I tell you? The Sinop men went at one another over their shares of the profits. They broke into two factions, and one wiped out the other."

Ismail didn't ask: "What'll happen now?" He knew the murderers would be held in the dungeon for a month and then come back up to carry on their business as usual.

"But why would Gay Ihsan want to kill me?"

"The lieutenant told the men that if they also got rid of the Communist in the fight, they'd get a lighter sentence. These Communist bastards, he said, are the archenemies of the state. They first assigned the job to Gay Ihsan, but when he attacked Murtaza first and got knifed, the lieutenant himself went for you."

Things didn't turn out the way Ismail thought. After a quick hearing, the lieutenant and the others were shipped off to Çankırı Prison. The new attorney general was said to be a reformer.

"Honestly, wife, I'm ashamed to eat the food you bring me."

"Why should you be ashamed?"

"People are dying of hunger inside."

"Outside it's not much better, Ismail. But what can we do? And Emine cooked you the *tarhana* soup with her own hands today."

Emine wears a blue ribbon in her curly black hair.

"Eat, father. And I used lots of red pepper and ground meat, too."

Hunger in prison. From the "Adams" ward, they cart out one or two bodies every week. First, they swell up like drums, then deflate and die. And the peasant visitors now carry skinnier bundles.

Ismail stepped outside the shop. A sunny day. He took a deep breath. He looked across the way. The "Adams" inmates, all in tatters, with a peasant or two among them, were down on all fours below the Genoese wall, eating the fresh grass, not with their hands but right from the ground like animals. No pushing or shoving, they graze like sad animals.

The Twenty-Fourth Line

AHMET OPENED his eyes. Ismail knelt by the food cupboard, busy with something. And the gas lamp burned.

"Ismail, is it still night? Did you just get back from work?"

"I haven't gone yet. Sleep. It's early."

"What're you doing there?"

"I'm making soup. *Tarhana*. It'll be good in the early morning."

Ahmet said: "Thank you." He didn't say he had no appetite. He checked himself.

"How are you?"

He didn't say, "Awful." He checked himself again. "I'm okay."

"Let me see if you have a fever."

"No. It's low-grade . . ."

Ismail touched Ahmet's forehead.

He didn't say, "You're burning up." He checked himself.

"It's come down. Not all the way, but it's down. I'll get you some medicine."

"Okay."

He didn't say, "What good will medicine do?" He checked himself.

They ate the soup Ismail had made. Ahmet tried not to show his distaste for it.

"I like it hot, Ahmet. I guess I went overboard with the red pepper."

"Maybe a little."

"Do you want an aspirin?"

"Yeah, give me a couple."

"Too many are bad for the heart, they say."

Ahmet did not say, "So what if I hurt my heart?" He took two aspirins. And I'm shivering—if I don't get hold of myself, my teeth will chatter.

Ahmet wrapped the blanket around him and sat on the bed.

"Ismail, I'm going to tell you something I've never told anyone—*couldn't* ever tell anyone."

"Brother, wouldn't it be better if you just lay down and rested?"

"No, no. You never talk about your mother or the women you love. But, you know, I babble."

"It's just your nature. But don't wear yourself out . . ."

"The Chinese, the Chinese at the university in Moscow."

"I know."

"A group of them went back to their country, Si-Ya-U among them. The people in the group before them were arrested as soon as they crossed the border, and their heads were chopped off— all of them, you know?"

"I know."

"Three girls were in the first group. You know?"

"Why wouldn't I know, brother? I understand perfectly well."

"I meant, am I making myself clear?"

"Perfectly."

"We know they chopped off the heads of the people in the first group with meat cleavers. We had a meeting. To protest. What I mean is, Si-Ya-U knew all this, too."

"Of course, if you knew it."

"Si-Ya-U knew all this, too. We had a last meeting at the club that night. Speeches were made. They would leave the next day. After the meeting, Anushka said, 'I'm going out with Si-Ya-U tonight.'"

They left. Si-Ya-U came back late. I pretended to sleep. I didn't ask anything. He didn't go to bed. He packed his stuff. I got up. We hugged. He left.

"You mean they chopped off his head, too?"

"I don't know. And I returned to Turkey with Kerim not long after that. Give me a cigarette."

But I don't really want it. My mouth tastes sour.

"Rest. You're tired."

"No. I'm going to tell you."

Why do I need to tell him this? I don't know. Maybe because I dreamed of Anushka all night.

I went to Anushka's that night. I had looked for her in the office that day. She hadn't come in. I entered her room. She was lying on the couch.

"Are you sick?"

"A little out of sorts."

I sat on the edge of the sofa.

"Shall I make tea?"

"No."

"You're in pain, of course. So am I. They won't catch him. If they caught everyone coming in . . ."

"Let it go."

"Why snap at me?"

"I'm not snapping."

"Whatever."

Suddenly I asked—this always happens to me, before I can decide whether I should say something, a demon gets in me and I blurt it out, out of the blue: "Did you and Si-Ya-U walk the boulevard last night?"

Blue eyes suddenly turn black with malice: "We went to Marusa's"

"The Marusas are in Rostov."

"I have the key to the house."

"Where? Show me."

Her sable eyebrows knit tight: "Do I have to account to you?"

"N-o-o-o . . . What would you have to account for? What did you do there?"

"We slept."

Two awls bored through my eyes.

"What do you mean you 'slept'?"

"I mean we slept. Like you and me."

"You're lying."

"Why would I lie?"

"Why did you do it?"

Anushka said, with a strange, disdainful, forced smile: "That's the stupidest question I've ever heard."

I grabbed my hat and ran. This street and that, this boulevard and the other. I went to the movies, not once or twice but four or five times. I left them all in the middle.

"Well, brother, that's tough."

"It's not easy."

"And then?"

"Then we didn't talk for two weeks. Wherever I saw Anushka, I ran."

"Then?"

"Then one night she dropped in out of the blue. After Si-Ya-U left, Kerim moved in with me. 'Hi, guys,' she said. As if nothing had happened. I pulled a long face. Kerim knew nothing, but he knew I'd been on edge for a while."

"Anushka," he asked, "what's with Ahmet here?"

"I don't know. Ask him."

"I ask, but he won't say."

"Maybe he doesn't want to tell the truth, that's why. Not everyone tells the truth like you do. (She touched his hair.) Ahmet and I will be spending the holidays at my aunt's dacha. My vacation starts in two weeks. And the university goes on break, too. Right, Ahmet?"

Kerim: "Man, why'd you keep this a secret from me? I'll visit you on Sundays."

"Of course, Kerimushka, and Marusa will be back from Rostov by then; you can come together. Ah, what was I going to say? I came to get you, Ahmet. I have two tickets to the Little Theater."

As we walked down Tverskoy Boulevard, I came to a stop.

"I'm not going to the theater. And what's this about the dacha?"

"I spoke with my aunt. She'll give us a room."

"Thank her. But I'm going to the university's dacha."

"Walk."

She took my arm. We're walking past Grand Yeliseyef Market, not talking.

"The long face—it's from that?"

"I'm an Easterner."

"Si-Ya-U, a man maybe going to his death, who's hopelessly in love with all his heart. If I sleep with him one night, if I make him happy for one night, is that such a crime?"

"We just don't agree on this, Anushka. Let go of my arm."

"Are you sure I slept with Si-Ya-U?"

Stunned, I stopped.

"Stopping every two steps must also be an Eastern custom. Please walk."

"Did you sleep with him or not?"

"Let's say I did, let's say I didn't. Does this have anything to do with my loving you?"

"Doesn't it?"

"I didn't sleep with him."

"You're lying."

"Then I slept with him."

"Don't drive me insane."

"Then I didn't sleep with him."

"Brother, did she or didn't she sleep with him?"

"I don't know, Ismail. To this day, I don't know."

"Didn't you go to Marusa, or whatever her name is, and ask?"

"The Marusas live in a two-room, run-down wooden house. They'd all gone to Rostov."

"Maybe she didn't sleep with him but just said it because you got her mad. From what you say, she's a stubborn, headstrong girl. Maybe she didn't sleep with him."

"Maybe. And maybe she did." Ahmet took a deep breath: "Like my rabies thing. Maybe the dog was rabid, maybe he wasn't. Maybe I should have gone to Istanbul, maybe I shouldn't. Maybe I'll get rabies, maybe . . ."

"Stop this rabies talk. You don't look like you're getting rabies."

"Today is number twenty-four. Draw the twenty-fourth line, Ismail."

"Let it go, brother."

"Draw it."

Ismail drew the twenty-fourth line on the door.

"Try to sleep. I'll get some medicine. There must be something besides aspirin to bring down a fever."

Ismail left.

Ismail left prison in '43.

The day before, Neriman told him: "I won't meet you at the prison door. You come to the house as if you were returning from work. Emine and I will meet you as if you were coming home from work. Don't forget the address; write it down somewhere."

His release took a while. Late that afternoon, Ismail gathered up his suitcase and tools, said his goodbyes, and stepped outside.

He walked a few steps. It was like all the Anatolian towns he'd known. Because he had been brought to the prison at night, he really hadn't seen the place. He turned left at Town Hall Square. He went to the town gardens. At the center, mounted on a cement base, stood a bust of Atatürk. And a clock—in the cement stand they'd inset an alarm clock, a common alarm clock like everyone has. Of course, it didn't work. He turned into the back streets smelling of cow dung and steaming bulgur. Stone mortars sat outside the doors of the houses. I'll visit the cemetery tomorrow, he thought. He entered a narrow street, the yards closed off with high wood fences. Here's our house: two stories, wooden, the downstairs whitewashed, the upstairs unfinished. Black wooden beams holding up the roof. Before he had a chance to knock on the door, it opened. He found Emine in his arms.

"Wait, girl. The suitcases . . ."

"She has sat by the window since morning, waiting for you."

Ismail stepped inside. He took off his shoes and put on slippers.

"Welcome, husband."

"Hello, wife."

"Did they work you hard at the factory today?"

"Same as ever."

The house has two rooms. The kitchen is in the yard, along with the bathroom. One of the rooms is a parlor, with divans and firm pillows against the walls. The kilim at the center glows like the sun. And there's a small writing desk with a chair.

"We eat on the floor, off the tray."

"Good."

On the wall hangs a picture of Ismail in a cap, enlarged from a passport-size photo.

"I'll have Emine's picture enlarged, too, but the photographer is waiting for paper from Istanbul."

"Enlarge yours, too. The one I have."

"Let's all take a picture together."

"Can we, father?"

"Yes, daughter."

They went into the bedroom: more divans, and a brass bed with four balls on four posts. On the blanket, a snow-white embroidered cover. In one corner, a dresser and a mirror. Ah, the nightstand by the bed! Ahmet had Master Zeki in prison build the dresser and the nightstand.

"Father, I'll sleep with mother, on the cushions."

"I'm sleeping here tonight."

Neriman blushed. "I'll make a bed for Emine in the other room."

"I won't sleep in the other room."

"Look, Emine, daughter, we'll settle this in advance. I don't like stubborn, difficult children."

As they ate in the parlor, off the sparkling copper tray and newly plated copper bowls, Ismail said: "Would you like a brother, Emine—younger than you, who would look up to you?"

"Right now, father?"

"Well, not right now, but who knows, he just might come one day."

"Yes, I want him to come. First, we'll shave his head to get rid of the lice, then I'll sew clothes for him."

Ismail looked at Neriman sitting across from him. Her cheeks flushed red. He just noticed her dress.

"What a beautiful dress, sister. Stand up and let me see you."

Neriman got up and stood before him.

"Do you really like it?"

"Like it! Did you make it yourself?"

"Who else? I'm sewing even for the governor's wife."

After dinner, Ismail turned on the radio, the portable Neriman had brought from Istanbul. "Let's hear from Moscow."

He listened to the broadcast.

"We're on the march—stop us if you can. What were the poet's words?

> This army is your army, this army is my army,
> This army is ours, the workers' army. . . .

Wow. Life's good, sister."

Neriman repeated in her guttural voice: "Life's good, brother."

Ismail realized he hadn't kissed Neriman yet. He tried to hug her.

"Wait. Not in front of Emine."

"And when does this daughter of ours sleep? Kids need to go to bed early."

"I'm not sleepy, father."

"What did we say? What was our deal, sister?"

Neriman put Emine to bed. She kissed her cheeks. As she walked into the bedroom, she whispered: "Sit with her awhile."

Ismail sat on the divan by Emine's bed. "Close your eyes."

Emine closed her eyes.

"If you go to sleep right now, I'll buy you a pinwheel tomorrow."

Emine opened her eyes: "What's a pinwheel, father?"

"Forget the pinwheel. I'll buy you a doll."

Emine shut her eyes tight.

Ismail took off his jacket, folded it, and laid it on the white-covered divan. He stood up, tiptoed to the table, and blew out the lamp. Emine was sound asleep.

Ismail opened the bedroom door quietly. A little oil lamp was burning. Neriman lay in bed, the satin quilt pulled up to her neck, her big black eyes full of fear and curiosity. Ismail thought, "Should I turn off the light?" He turned it off and got undressed.

Softly, Neriman surrendered.

THE END OF THE TWENTY-FOURTH LINE IN IZMIR

ISMAIL RETURNED to the cottage. Ahmet lay on his back, staring at the ceiling.

"How do you feel?"

"Better."

"I got you Primidone. They said caffeine and urotropin are also good."

"Who'd you say you bought these for?"

"For myself. They sell them over the counter. Now, take these. One of this and this and this."

Ahmet swallowed the pills.

"You know, your uncle Şükrü Bey has fled."

"No!"

"Honest, I just heard it. Two days ago, he ran off to Europe."

"How?"

"Nobody knows. They say he collaborated with the British. Because he did business with them."

"He's a collaborator, pure and simple."

"His wife is your real relative, right?"

"She's my aunt."

"She wouldn't open the door to the police. She wanted to see a search warrant. The police didn't have a search warrant. They pressured her. Your aunt said, 'I'll shoot you from this window!' I like that woman, brother."

"That's how the women are on my mother's side. When my mother was pregnant with me, Sultan Hamid's agents raided our seaside house in Üsküdar. My grandfather knew the poet Namık Kemal. He was younger than them, but he loved both Namık Kemal and, especially, Ziya Pasha. Some manuscripts—poems, maybe—were stored in the house. My mother grabbed all the papers, stuffed them under the mattress, and got in bed. When the agents burst into her room, she screamed, 'Get out, you pigs. How can you walk into a good Muslim woman's bedroom? If you don't leave right now, I'll shoot.' She took my father's gun from her nightstand. That gun is still around. A rusty six-shooter. I asked, 'Father, why do you hold on to this thing?' He said, 'To scare off thieves.' But he doesn't know how to use a gun any more than I do. And you know where his fear of thieves comes from? Once, long ago, he saw a picture in *Illustrated Journal*. At midnight, thieves break into a Paris apartment and butcher the husband and wife in their bedroom. Of course, it's not just because of the picture. My father is as cowardly as my mother is brave."

Ahmet doesn't know his father was taken to police headquarters in Istanbul, questioned about his son's whereabouts, and roughed up. And Ahmet also doesn't know that, although his father knew he was in Izmir, he said nothing.

"Back when I was in Moscow, they fired my father from his job because of me. He could have been appointed an ambassador. Now he's working for a thug as a hotel manager."

"Did the pills help?"

"Do they work that fast? But they will. Thanks, Ismail."

I know the medicines won't do any good. What help is Primidone for rabies? But am I sure I have rabies, and all these aches and pains and the fever are symptoms of it? Am I a hundred-percent sure? Was Petrosian a hundred-percent sure he had cancer? He wasn't sure—he knew, but he wasn't sure, he didn't believe it a hundred percent. And when you believe . . . Am I a hundred-percent sure Petrosian killed himself? When I'm a hundred-percent sure, when I believe I'll go rabid, I'll take all twenty sleeping pills, and . . .

"Ismail, I ran out of sleeping pills."

"I'll get some. But watch out you don't get hooked."

Why didn't I think of this sooner? Rather than living through hell. Okay. But when? Tomorrow night? I'll wait a little longer.

It's the matter of the hundred percent, the matter of grasping at a twig when you're drowning at sea.

"The old ones don't help me any more; get the strongest pills you can."

The Seventh Line in Anushka's Dacha

"What are these, Ahmet?"

Anushka saw the seventh line I drew on the back of the door opening to the glassed-in porch of the dacha.

"Our seventh day, Anushka. That means we have thirteen more days."

"And then?"

"And then, you know. Your leave is over, my vacation ends, and we return to Moscow."

I'm lying. Not about going back to Moscow but pretending nothing will happen when we return. A week or, at most, ten days after we get back to Moscow, Kerim and I are off. Istanbul, here we come! But we won't have a going-away party like the one the Chinese had for Si-Ya-U. Our situation is different. We must get back into Turkey before anyone knows we're coming. In any case, the police will know it the next day, because both Kerim and I will openly work for *Aydınlık*. The thing is to get to Istanbul in one piece. Only a couple of people from the Comintern and our Party representative know we're going to Istanbul. It seems strange to keep this from Anushka and act like I'll be with her for a couple more years, at least; more than strange, it's wrong, but what can I do?

"Why count the days we have left, Ahmet? When I'm watching a real good play, I don't think about how much longer it will last. I watch it as if it'll never end."

"Is the play we're watching—or, rather, acting in—'real good'?"

"Very good. But I don't like the word 'acting.' I don't know about you, but I'm not acting."

"You're not a spectator, are you?"

"No, but here we're not watching or acting in a play; we're living it."

Anushka looked out through the open door of the terrace, smiling, at the sunny white beeches and the tall pines. Then her smile—slowly, as if her lipstick (she doesn't wear lipstick, but similes are never wrong), as if her lipstick was wiped off with an invisible handkerchief—her smile disappeared.

"I don't see how I can live without you, Ahmet. A year later, three years later, you'll leave. And you won't come back."

"Why not? You never know, I might come back."

"You *won't* come back. You'll be dead for me. I don't know how I'll live . . ."

"Didn't you just say you never think about when the play will end?"

"I guess I think about it sometimes."

I hugged her and kissed her lips.

Anushka's dacha or, rather, her aunt's dacha is a forty-five minute train ride from Moscow. The forest . . . The forest holds lots of dachas. Ours is fifteen minutes from the station. When it rains, and it's rained once since we came, it takes real acrobatics to get there on the forest roads. Such mud! The dacha is a single story and is built from round pine logs, like Russian peasants' cabins. Three rooms. Anushka's aunt, Mariya Andreyevna, let us have one of them. Her husband died in 1915, at the front in the Caucasus.

Petya delivered us milk from his village an hour away. His hair like wool, his shirt open at the neck, beltless and barefoot, he was a sweet little boy. He must have been about fourteen.

We got our towels and headed for the lake. Anushka keeps bending down to pick things—I don't know the Turkish for them, and I can never remember the Russian—things like tiny strawberries or currants. When she has a handful, she says: "Open your mouth."

I open and she stuffs them in.

It's like eating weeds, but I don't say anything, because I like Anushka's offerings.

The lakeshore is crowded.

"The Nepmen are early today," says Anushka.

Lots of women in their underwear, most of them fat, and a whole slew of noisy, naked kids have gathered in groups. Some sit under umbrellas—I mean, regular rain umbrellas—and some sunbathe, on their backs or face down. And some go swimming in the lake. The Nepmen rent dachas in the forest. Evenings, they get all dressed up and go to the train station to stroll up and down the wooden platform.

We find a spot, not too crowded, and undress. Anushka's body, with her thickish legs and blue swimsuit, dazzles me again.

We're swimming side by side. I see her head wrapped in a white scarf and, now and then, her arms splashing the water, glistening in the sun.

We lie on our backs on the lakeshore. I hold Anushka's hand.

"Anushka, you're so beautiful."

"That's the fourth time today."

"I'll say it all day, twenty more times, till we go to bed tonight."

"I don't like it when you talk mushy."

I look at the people lying on the lakeshore. I see the priest's daughter. She's very attractive, and she knows it. All the young men from the dachas and the village are after her. I remember the beach in Batum. And the women's sea baths in Üsküdar: a little offshore, all four sides covered with wooden fences driven into the sea floor. I could hear the women screaming inside. I remember Aunt Cemile saying, "I used to catch you between my legs and bathe you in the seaside house." I tell Anushka.

"You always make the most normal things seem shameful. You're disgusting."

I walk around in something like warm-up pants that I wear over my underpants, not just in the house but sometimes on the station platform, too. Most of the young men from the city go around in them.

We return to the dacha. Mariya Andreyevna has graying, light-blond hair. Her eyes and legs look like Anushka's.

"A letter came, kids."

It's a letter is from Kerim and Marusa. The message: We'll be there next Sunday. Anushka is happy. So am I.

Anushka lies under the awesomest, tallest pine tree in the front yard. She opens her books. She's studying. She'll be an engineer. I take out my paints and start a portrait of Mariya Andreyevna.

The First Line at
Police Headquarters

Late one night they arrested Ismail at home and took him to
headquarters. Neriman was two months pregnant.

Istanbul police headquarters are in Sansarian Khan, on a
quiet back street between Eminönü and Sirkeci. The street has
other office buildings but no shops with windows. Sansarian
Khan once belonged to a rich Armenian. Four stories, with a
stone-paved courtyard at the center. Two stairways. The Political
Division, Fourth Bureau: the Communist Desk is on the top
floor. When you reach the top-floor landing, you face a door
marked with two crescents, which mean "No Entry."

It was winter, one of those hard winters that hit Istanbul
every so many years. The stone courtyard was packed with
various motor vehicles. They climbed to the fourth floor, opened
the door with the two crescents, and walked in. The corridor
leading to the chief's office was lined with detainees. They sat
on chairs lined up side by side, their heads bowed. A policeman
paced before them. As Ismail passed, those sitting on the chairs
glanced at him. Ismail recognized some of them, some he didn't.
If the men had spilled out into the corridors, it must have been
a big round-up. They entered the bureau chief's office. Oilcloth
armchairs, a wide desk. The chief sat at the table: light-brown
complexion, heavy-set. Four or five plainclothesmen stand
around. One is the commissioner. Ismail knows this very tall,
thin, dark man in glasses and two of the plainclothesmen. It's not
hard to recognize them. They all wear government-issue gray or
striped brown suits. They all wear dark-gray felt hats.

The bureau chief: "Ziya gave you the typewriter and stencils."

"I don't know anyone named Ziya. No one gave me any such
stuff. I've already said so at the station. You raided my house. If I
had such things, you'd have found them."

"You gave them to Kerim."

"I don't know anyone named Kerim."

The chief asked the same questions in different sentences. Ismail gave the same answers.

The chief: "Bring in the sticks."

One of the men left.

The chief said things like "This isn't the first time you're here; you know what's going to happen. Those who talked, talked, and they told us where Ziya and Kerim are. Don't make it hard on yourself or us." Ismail fixed his eyes on the red-hot coals burning in the iron stove. His head feels like an engine spinning out of control: if they have men in the corridors, this is a big round-up. Who caved in? They haven't got Ziya and Kerim. Other than me, who knows where they are? The man came back with the dogwood sticks—all gradations of thin and thick.

"Lie down."

With all his strength, Ismail lunged at the commissioner in glasses standing next to him. This was his method. He knew he'd be down in an instant, but just to lie down with no resistance hurt his pride. This was one point. The other was that, even if he got beaten harder, he felt more powerful for having made the first attack.

Ismail couldn't tell whether the chief got up from his table at that point; everyone in the room jumped him at once. Slaps, fists, curses, and kicks—he was brought down. He flailed around on the floor like a fish trying to escape a net. As he rolled his head right and left, he saw the red light in the iron stove's mica front cover. The red light flashed in his eyes, on and off. They put the *falaka* on his feet with great speed and dexterity. Two men sat on his chest. With great speed and efficiency, they took off his shoes. The chief held the stick: "Are you going to talk?"

"I have nothing to say."

The chief started beating Ismail's feet. Then two sticks, then three. Ismail feels no pain. He feels nothing but rage. He doesn't scream. He doesn't swear. Who said I got it from Ziya and gave it to Kerim? The light bulb on the ceiling burns inside his eyes. They didn't remove his socks so the blood wouldn't spill on the floor. Ismail knows: blood will collect under his nails, and then the nails will fall off. They took off the *falaka*. A bucket of water stands by. They picked him up by the arms, slapping him when he struggled, and stuck his feet in the bucket. The water was ice-cold. Still supporting him by the arms, they made him walk. After a while, footsoles get numb and feel nothing. Cold water and walking seem to send new blood to the feet, and they started to feel again. They laid Ismail down again. Put on the *falaka* again. The sticks came down again. Ismail could tell the commissioner's stick from the others. After bringing down the stick, the thug also slid it off. The chief no longer beat. Ismail started screaming. The pain was unbearable. The chief wiped the sweat off his face and paused the beating: "Are you going to talk?"

"I have nothing to say."

The sticks came down again, one after another. Ismail made out that he was screaming at the top of his lungs. How long had he been in that room? He didn't know. Maybe two hours, maybe three. The electric bulb faded out. Dawn outside.

"Take him away."

Two people took Ismail by the arms. He couldn't step on his feet. They dragged him out of the room. On his way out, he saw the early winter morning through the windows. They walked down the corridor. Those on the chairs didn't hide their stares. Some tried something like a smile, a mixture of a little fear, a little sorrow, curiosity, and brotherhood.

Still supporting Ismail under the arms, they took him down the stairs, his shoes dangling from his hands. His legs dragged behind him as if broken at the knees. Paling light bulbs and winter dawn light everywhere. Downstairs, they opened a door next to the misdemeanors ward and shoved Ismail inside.

A stone cell. Cement floor. The walls soiled whitewash. They let go of him. He collapsed on the floor. They straightened him up. With great dexterity, they undressed him and left him in his underwear, his long underpants tied at the ankles, his shoes still in his hands. He sits against the wall. A dull light bulb hangs from the ceiling. The soles of his feet burn as if branded with a hot iron. The plainclothesmen took his clothes, shut the door, locked it, and left. And it was freezing-cold inside. His teeth chattered. Like a fisherman, he slapped his arms around his body on both sides, his bare chest and belly all goosebumps. God, these guys are worse than the soldiers, and at least the bilge was steamy-hot. He suddenly felt he wasn't alone in the cell. He turned around. A man sat perched on something like an orange crate. Ismail saw his fringe of a beard through the raised collar of his overcoat. He wore a beret. He stared at Ismail, bug-eyed, hands in his coat pockets. Ismail thought, "He isn't one of us."

Ismail: "Hello."

"Peace be with you."

"Hope all's well."

"Thank you."

"Been here long?"

"A week."

"Why'd they throw you in?"

"False accusation."

"Yes, but accused of what, brother?"

"Supposedly I printed and sold Korans in Arabic."

The guy didn't ask, "Why were you thrown inside?" He closed his eyes. Ismail tried to stand up. No way. Stepping on his feet felt like walking on hot iron. And the blood filling his socks had dried.

"Brother, it's freezing in here."

The man with the fringe beard opened his eyes, looked at Ismail, and closed them.

Ismail got to his knees, with great difficulty and in great pain. Before long, his kneecaps froze. He sat back on his butt. Then he suddenly thought—and was frighteningly happy at the thought—to sit on his shoes.

The cell didn't have a window.

Ismail thought of the lines Ahmet drew on the door of the cottage in '25. He scratched a line on the whitewashed wall with his fingernails: the first line. Who all broke down? Arrests happening on this scale, and I didn't hear about them? Did they round up all those people in one night?

The door opened. A cop, with bread and a paper bag in his hand: "Father."

The man on the crate opened his eyes. He stepped down. He took the bread and the paper bag. As he was settling back down on the crate, the door shut. The man opened the paper bag: black olives.

"My son."

"Who?"

"The man who brought the bread and olives."

"Well, if your son's a cop, you'll get out soon."

The man spoke with his mouth full: "What can he do? Falsely accused. An accusation like this—if the seven nations got together and studied it for seven weeks, they'd never get to the bottom of it."

The bearded man finished his bread and olives, got up, walked over to the can in the corner, squatted down, and pissed. He climbed back on his perch.

It must have been toward noon when the door opened again. The bearded man's son handed his father meatballs wrapped in pita bread. And a bottle of water. The guy ate the meatballs and drank the water. He burped and asked Ismail: "Don't you have anyone? If no one takes you food, you'll meet your maker here from hunger."

"I'll meet him from freezing first."

It must have been toward nightfall when the door opened again. His son gave the man bread and pastrami. Ismail was getting hungry. Neriman must have brought something. He banged on the door. They opened it. A policeman—not the son of the beard—incredibly bow-legged, amazingly standing somehow, and needing a shave: "Hey, you—what's the matter? Why're you making a racket?"

Before Ismail could answer, the man on the crate said: "It wasn't me, it was that man."

"What does he want?"

"Didn't anyone bring me food?"

"We'll find out."

The door closed.

"Don't bang on the door. If anyone took you food, they'll give it to you."

Ismail looked blankly at the man picking his teeth with a toothpick—where did he find it?

The door opened. The commissioner with the glasses and someone else. They threw Ismail's clothes at him.

"Didn't anyone bring me food?"

"Your wife did. We turned her away."

"Why?"

"You can go without food a few days."

They pulled the door shut and left. Ismail managed to get dressed. After he put on his clothes and warmed up a bit, he started shivering. He was shaking as if shocked by an electric current.

He spent that night sitting on his shoes, his head buried in his jacket collar—they didn't give him back his coat. He woke up once with an unbearable thirst. The beard, roosted on his crate, snored away. Ismail dragged himself over to him. He took a swig from the water bottle by the crate, then another. Then all of it.

The next morning he woke up to the screams of the beard: "You drank my water!"

"I was very thirsty."

"You can't have food or water. I'll report you."

A little later the door opened, and the man's son brought bread and olives again.

"Ibrahim, this man drank my water last night."

"So what, father? I'll get you fresh water."

"They told me he's forbidden to eat or drink."

"A sip of water doesn't hurt anything."

"You know best. But I was falsely accused, and you can get in trouble, too."

The bearded man's son didn't answer. He was a blond young man. His uniform and hat were spotless. He took the bottle and left and returned with water a little later.

Ismail scratched the second line on the wall.

It must have been around noon when the beard's son brought him meatballs in pita bread. A little later, the door opened. The commissioner with glasses, without looking at Ismail, told the man on the crate: "Hodja, don't give this man any food, or you'll end up fasting, too."

"Of course I won't."

Ismail had vast experience in solitary confinement. He could pass months inside four walls. There was no talking with the beard. Ismail counted him among the inanimate objects in the room. He studied the man. He sits just like that, roosting on his crate. When's he going to get up and walk around? His nails are very long and very dark. His fingers are yellow like wax. And his nose is crooked. I'm going to count up to a thousand, and the man is going to get up. He counted to a thousand. The man still sat just like that. I'm going to count up to three thousand, and he's going to close his eyes. The man closed his eyes at 2,264. How many watts is that electric bulb? 25, tops. Like the one in our bathroom. Is that a bedbug crawling on the ceiling? How does a bedbug get in here? I'm counting up to ten thousand, and the man will open his eyes. He counted, but the man didn't open his eyes. How many centimeters is Emine— is she up to a meter? No. We have to measure her. Did they turn Neriman away without taking the food? Do they take the food but not give it to me? They wouldn't have turned her away without taking the food. They took it and treated themselves to it. Bastards! Sons of bitches! Not to feel cold—don't think of the cold.

The door opened. The cop gave his father the night's provisions: tahini helvah and bread. The guy scarfed it down. The oily crumbs of the helvah stick to his beard. He knocked on the door. They opened.

"I need to do my big toilet," he said.

Ismail: "Me, too."

They first took out the fanatic and brought him back. To Ismail: "You take the urine can, too."

Ismail stood up, in pain, to get the urine can. He still couldn't step on his feet. The cop took his arm.

In the bathroom, Ismail put his mouth to the faucet and drank his fill of water. When he got back, the beard was pacing back and forth.

Ismail counted the man's steps: 552. The man perched on his crate again. He buried his beard in his coat and slept. Ismail knew: in places like this, you don't think much about the people you love. You can't think about the outside. You have to think about bad people, things that make you mad. They'll call us in for questioning tonight. Like it or not. His heart pounding, he waited for hours for the door to open, but it didn't.

His stomach growled from hunger. Brother, I've always had a big appetite.

The next day—morning, noon, and night—the man on the crate again received food and drink. Ismail tried not to look at him when he ate. His feet hurt less. And maybe the cold broke, or maybe he got used to it. He scratched the third line.

The next day, as the fanatic ate the meatballs—they smelled delicious, and the pita was clearly warm—he said: "They taste so good. My son must get them from that joint in Babıali."

Ismail could barely keep from swearing at the bastard, starting with his mother. They didn't call him in for questioning that night or the night after.

Ismail scratched the fifth line.

The man keeps eating in front of Ismail, wolfing down the meatballs, helvah, olives, pastrami, and pita bread. He picks his teeth. He spits. He belches. "God is good," he says, and stuffs his face.

Ismail scratched the sixth line. He lay on his back on the cement floor. The wretched inmates from the "Adams" ward, grazing below the Genoese walls, flashed before his eyes: fresh, green grass. He looked at the bastard eating his pastrami. . . . To jump the son of a bitch and snatch his pastrami. He felt nauseous, as if a knife was scraping his stomach lining. I'm getting used to hunger. The donkey, just when he was getting used to hunger, kicked up his heels. He tried to remember other Nasreddin Hodja jokes. He couldn't think of a single one. He scratched the seventh line. In these seven days, what he has seen, heard, felt, smelled, thought—all the confusion resolved into three questions: Who said Ziya gave me the typewriter and the stencils? Who said I gave them to Kerim? When will the door open to take me to the *falaka*? The door didn't open that night, either.

The next day, as the bearded bastard gobbled up the meatballs from the joint in Babıali, Ismail emptied the urine can over the man's head. The man didn't understand what was happening to him. Then he ran to the door, banging and screaming. They came and handcuffed Ismail in the back, and that night they took him to a room on the fourth floor, littered with heaps of trash and rubbish, and without a word they beat him unconscious. Then they dragged him into one of the cells in the Political Division and locked him up by himself. Ismail again saw the people sitting in the corridor. But most of them were new. And the dentist Agop sat on one of the stools. His white hair glowed under the naked bulb.

The Twenty-Fifth Line in Izmir

When Ismail opened the door and entered the cottage, Ahmet was drawing the twenty-fifth line on the door. But, hearing someone fiddle with the lock, he pulled back.

"Hello. So you're on your feet. How's the fever?"

"I think it's down."

"I brought a thermometer. Why didn't we think of this before, brother? Try this."

Ahmet put in the thermometer: 100.5.

"Good, good, it's coming down. You just caught a cold, that's all."

Ismail wasn't sure about this, and neither was Ahmet. But Ahmet grasped at this possibility: "I think I have the flu. Is the flu going around?"

"Of course."

(He's lying.)

"Half the workers in the factory are out with it."

(Lie.)

"How's your appetite?"

"Good, Ismail."

(He's lying.)

"I could wolf down a lamb at one sitting. Roast lamb."

(He's lying.)

"I couldn't find lamb, but I bought a roast chicken."

"Thank you. Bless you."

Ahmet worked on the chicken, each bite growing bigger and bigger in his mouth.

"You don't feel as sore, right?"

"Maybe just a little."

"It's a cold. It'll take its time."

"The flu."

"Like I said, half the workers in the factory."

"I don't scream at night now, do I, Ismail?"

"Not lately."

"Good."

"Yes."

"You told everyone I went to Istanbul, right?"

"That's what we all decided . . . There was no need to tell them—but it's hard to tell you anything, brother."

"Good. It's better if they think I'm in Istanbul. I mean, if something happens . . ."

"Nothing will happen. It happened, and it's over. Okay, off to bed." Ismail blew the "lights-out" whistle. "We lived next to an army barracks. I can whistle all the calls. Mess call. The call to attack."

"I just thought of something. If you go to Moscow someday, Ismail, look up Anushka—go find her."

"Maybe you'll go before me and find her yourself."

I thought, "I'm going somewhere else with twenty sleeping pills." And I felt sorry for myself, so sorry . . .

"When you go to Moscow, maybe five or ten years from now, Anushka will have settled down, with kids and stuff. With an engineer in some factory. Maybe the head engineer. I see before my eyes how she'll look ten or fifteen years from now. She'll look like her aunt: graying hair, heavier, and in love with strawberry jam. Her legs a little thicker. I'll give you the address of their dacha. Keep it somewhere."

"Yes, yes. But I blew lights out."

They went to bed. The motor continued *dum-dum-da-dum-dum.*

The Tenth Line in
Anushka's Dacha

We're having breakfast on the glassed-in porch, Mariya Andreyevna and I. Strawberry jam, the milk Petya delivered, oatmeal bread. Anushka hasn't appeared yet.

Mariya Andreyevna asked me something I didn't in the least expect, and she asked it in a low voice, as if she didn't want Anushka to hear: "Are you and Anushka going to get married? I mean, are you going to register at Zaks?"

What could I say?

"Certainly," I said.

"Good, good. She can go to Turkey with you. Because you'll return to your country one day."

"Sure."

"If you can't go back together, she can follow afterwards. To be man and wife legally is good. Isn't Zaks Soviet law?"

"Certainly."

Anushka came in and sat down. Mariya Andreyevna changed the subject: "I'll go to the market, sell some strawberries, and buy semolina—if I can find any."

Mariya Andreyevna owns strawberry fields. About twenty square meters. And this year's crop was good.

Nepmen families walk across the way. Sometimes Anushka and I walked through the streets in Moscow to see how many Nepmen shops had opened, how many had closed. Government bookstores have opened in most of the closed Nepmen shops.

Mariya Andreyevna: "I'll go pick strawberries."

Anushka bites into the oatmeal bread spread with jam, her white teeth flashing. Just to say something, I ask: "Do you know how to shoot a gun?"

"Yes, I do."

I'm surprised. "I don't."

"So?"

"Don't you disapprove that I don't?"

"No-o-o."

"Where did you learn to shoot? How?"

"After my father was shot before my eyes, I said I should learn to use a gun."

"And?"

"After my mother died of typhus in Siberia, I joined the partisans."

"You never told me this."

"There's nothing to tell. For six or seven months, I was useful to them."

"How? Tell me."

"Some other time. Now, off to the lake to swim! March!"

I got up. *Pravda* caught my eye. I picked it up. Yesterday's paper: 12 June 1924. In China, YU-PEY-FU is slaughtering the union leaders. They hanged the director of the Railway Union.

"What's wrong?"

"Terror in China."

Anushka snatched the paper from my hands. "Where?"

"Here."

She read but said nothing. She put the paper down on the table. "Let's go."

We headed for the lake. The mosquitos are horrendous. I'm walking and slapping myself on the chest, on the neck. Anushka is oblivious to them.

"Don't they bite you?"

"I guess my flesh is not as sweet as yours."

I keep remembering what Mariya Andreyevna said. It's impossible to go to Turkey with Anushka. But her coming later? Equally impossible.

We're walking side by side. The three of us, side by side: Anushka, separation, and me.

"Listen to the flute's lament, it grieves its separation."

"What're you mumbling, Ahmet?"

"There's a great poet, a mystic, but he's really great. Mevlana Rumi—I'm mumbling his lines."

I translated it into Russian for Anushka. And I explained its mystical meaning. The flute is made of a reed; it's broken off from a reed. So when you play it, it mourns its separation. Man is a fragment of the Universal—God, that is—and he's been torn away, separated from it, and he mourns this separation—I mean, the poet does.

"Read it in Turkish."

"It's really from Persian. They translated it into Turkish. I'll read you both."

I recited the lines.

"Both are very musical. I listen to you and Kerimushka when you speak Turkish. I like it and its rhythms."

"Why do you call him Kerimushka, when you haven't called me Ahmedushka even once?"

"True. That's very strange. Sometimes I call you Ahmedushka to myself, but I can't say it out loud, to your face. Who knows why?"

We swam. Then we lay on our backs on the shore again, our shoulders touching. I held Anushka's hand.

"Do you miss your country, Istanbul?"

She asked this as if she wasn't talking to me. She withdrew her hand.

"Why did you take your hand away?"

"I don't know. Maybe so it would be easier for you to answer my question."

Without turning my head, I found and held Anushka's hand. Again she asked as if she wasn't talking to me: "Why don't you answer?"

"What's not to answer? Some days I don't think of my country at all, but then, sometimes, out of the blue, I can just smell it. I live in that aura for days, for weeks, homesick, in pain, sometimes on the verge of tears."

"I understand."

"Don't take your hand away."

"What kind of smell? What kind of love is this for you?"

"The smell of the sea, pine trees, the earth—not that. Not the love of geography. Although, of course, some scenes make my eyes burn with longing. But the smell of my country, my love for my country, my ties to my people . . . When I say my people, I mean . . ."

"I know, you don't mean bourgeois people . . ."

"No, not the bourgeoisie, they're not my people—and not Turks or Russians, or French, but just people."

"For me, too."

Our shoulders touched.

"If you could, would you go back to Istanbul tomorrow—or, I don't know, next week, next month?"

"Why Istanbul?"

"Where else?"

"Yes, probably Istanbul first."

"Do you want to go back? Today, right now, this instant? At this moment, do you want to be there? Why did you pull your hand away? It's fine. Don't touch me. Do you want to, Ahmedushka? Ahmedushka . . . I understand . . . You're right . . . Let's go. It's gotten cold suddenly."

We dressed in silence. I'm thinking: "Now? This instant? Yes and no."

On the way, I said to Anushka: "Let's stop by Bagritski's."

Bagritski was one of my favorite Russian poets. A fine, straight-talking man is like uncut wine.

He greeted us at his garden gate. He grinned with his toothless mouth—maybe he had teeth, but that was how I saw his smile.

"Welcome, Osman Pasha."

For some reason, he always called me Osman Pasha—after Gazi Osman Pasha, the leader of the Plevne campaign.

"Anushka—such beauty! You're like a sunny wheat field."

Among the many things I loved about Bagritski, the first was his revolutionary romanticism and manliness that turned trees, grass, locomotives, and even spring into a woman and knew how to caress her. Poets and painters shouldn't be neutered.

We step inside. His dacha is tiny. Half dark, it smells damp. Japanese fish swim in aquariums, birds sing in cages, but it feels as if the fish and birds swim and fly around freely in this half-dark. Around Bagritski, freedom walks around swinging its arms.

His wife, a little woman, made us tea.

Bagritski read us his new poems in his warm voice coming from far, far away, from very deep down. How I loved this man! I could have sat for days among his fish, birds, and poems, gazing at his brotherly eyes. Inside this half-dark room blew the light breezes of the Black Sea off the coast of Odessa.

We walked back, part of my heart still with Eduard Bagritski. Mariya Andreyevna has traded her strawberries for potatoes instead of semolina.

Now it's midnight. Anushka and I lie side by side. The windows are open, but the lace curtains are drawn. Against the mosquitos. We can't even turn on the lamp.

Anushka, naked, sleeps on her back. She breathes like a child, lightly puffing. Her hand is in mine. I no longer turn to gaze on her nakedness glistening under the moonlight streaming into the room. Something heavy, sticky, and pitch-black rises inside me, up to my chest. My heart is pounding again. I grip Anushka's hand tightly. I stare at the moon whitening the curtain. The thing rising up to my chest spreads to my legs and arms. Did Anushka sleep with Si-Ya-U or not? I don't know. I'll never know. I don't picture Marusa's room—I know the divan in Marusa's room—or their making love there. Maybe I suppress those images. I think of their closeness. For me, a man and a woman are closest, unconditionally, only at that moment. This closeness of Anushka with someone other than me will drive me out of my mind. But after I leave, Anushka will find another man anyway. She'll marry. Maybe they'll register at Zaks. True. But when I'm gone, when I'm totally not here, when I'm dead to Anushka. No, that's not it. It's more complicated. I let her hand go and stand up. I dress and walk out into the moonlit forest.

THE END OF THE
TWENTY-FIFTH LINE IN IZMIR

"ISMAIL."

Ismail didn't wake up.

Ahmet repeated, louder: "Ismail!"

"What? What happened? Did you call me?"

"Nothing happened. Forgive my rudeness."

"Tell me, brother—what's going on?"

"You forgot my sleeping pills."

"I couldn't get them. They need a prescription. Tomorrow I'll have a doctor I know write you a prescription. Try to sleep. Go on, count to five hundred."

"I'm sorry."

"Go on, go to sleep."

I was an ass to wake Ismail. I could have written him a note, "You forgot the sleeping pills," and put it on his clothes.

I toss and turn. Now I'm lying on my back. My two arms hang at my sides, like dead men's in their graves. Damn it. Is there a crematorium in Moscow? Is it better to be burned? Silly words. When I'm dead, if they want . . . But Engels asked to be cremated, and he wanted his ashes scattered on the ocean. And that's what they did. One of the wisest old men in the world and the youngest romantic. Engels. I have to sleep. There's nothing to do but sleep. I have to sleep . . .

Before I woke up to Ismail shaking me, I heard myself screaming as if strangling. I heard my own terrible scream. It felt like I had been screaming for hours. I couldn't place where I was. For a minute, I thought I was in Moscow, in Anushka's room, and then, for some reason, on the stone landing of the seaside house in Istanbul, then inside the hole, under the trapdoor.

"Wake up, brother!"

Ismail's hand is on my shoulder, shaking me. He's lit the lamp.

In his other hand he's holding something. For a split second I see what's in his hand, but then he puts his hand behind his back, to hide it from me.

"Don't be afraid, Ismail."

He's looking at me with four—that's what it feels like—wide-open eyes. "I'm not afraid. Why should I be afraid? Pull yourself together, brother. Do you want some water?"

"No."

"How do you feel?"

"Fine. Don't blow out the lamp."

Ismail went back to bed.

"Try to sleep."

"You, too."

But neither of us could sleep. We didn't talk but secretly watched each other, like hunters and their prey.

LINES AT THE ISTANBUL POLICE HEADQUARTERS

THEY THREW ISMAIL into a dark cell. These bastards are into darkness. The soldiers had left him in the dark, too. Ismail can tell whether it's day or night only when he walks down the hall to the bathroom. With his nails he scratches lines on the cell wall, but he can't see to count them. They don't call him in for questioning. Any minute now they'll call me, now they'll call and beat me—this waiting frays his nerves and wears him down. The bastards will wear me out and then take me. Now they give him the food from Neriman. At first, it was hard to find his mouth in the dark, but then he got used to it. Ismail knows they can hold him here for three, five, or nine months without questioning him. In the '28 arrests, Ziya used to say they held him a year after torturing him in his cell. They hadn't tortured Ismail much that time. Ziya used to say they stripped him to his underpants, handcuffed him from behind, and burned his chest, belly, and legs with their cigarettes. He used to show us the dark burn spots. And they pulled out two of his fingernails—his right pinkie and his left middle finger.

As Ismail walks down the corridor, he sees different people sitting on the chairs. Only the dentist Agop still sits on the same stool. He looks confused, as if drugged. Once, as they were walking Ismail past him, Agop fell off his stool. They picked him right up and mocked him, "Oh, Agop Effendi, here, make yourself comfortable," and sat him back on his stool. Ismail understood: they were torturing the dentist Agop with sleep deprivation. Sometimes they'll keep someone on his feet for days, with no sleep. Policemen will change shifts while guarding him. The minute you pass out, they jab you awake. You fall down like a stiff, and they stand you right back up. Because of his advanced age, I guess, they let Agop sit on a stool. Several days later, Ismail saw Agop fall down again. They picked him up again. About 27 days, no, 25, no, 27, Agop sits on the stool. He falls off, and he's put back on. When he falls, his head hits the floor; there's dried blood at the roots of his white hair, and his face is all cut and bruised.

On the fourth floor, outside the door with the double crescents, wait the mothers, wives, and sisters of the detainees.

After Ismail had been inside who-knows-how-many months, Neriman got sick. For a week, Osman Bey took Ismail his food. I'm a free man; they can't do anything to me. But when Ismail gets out this time, he should come to his senses. I'm not saying he should give up the cause, but he'll soon be a father. And Emine is like his daughter, too. I'm not saying he should give up, but he shouldn't always put himself on the front line.

Neriman met Kerim's sister outside the door with the two crescents. They arrested Kerim twenty-five days ago, two months after Ismail. Kerim's sister is old, plump, and friendly. And she runs up the stairs so fast, you'd think she was a girl of fourteen.

Neriman: "I ran into Kerim on the bus a month ago. He stood up in the front. I was so happy to see him. Before I could make my way up to him through the crowd, the bus stopped. There was no time to call 'Kerim!'—he jumped off. I got off, too. He's walking very fast, not looking behind him. I'm following him. He turns into a side street, going up a hill, and starts running. Then it hit me: he didn't want to see me."

Kerim's sister has a lunch box and four red roses. She's carried them from Sarıyer. She gave Neriman a rose: "Kerim grows these roses in the greenhouse he built with his own hands." Then she said: "When we leave here, they always follow us to see where we're going and who we're talking to. That's why Kerim ran from you. A pockmarked idiot here follows me everywhere. The other day, I dropped off the food here in the morning and left. The pock-face follows me. I go into the

Hazelnut Baths. I stay till the evening prayers, then go outside. And can you believe it? He's standing across the street from the baths! And it's snowing—the dog is shivering. Do they at least give our men the food we leave? Or do they stuff themselves with it?"

A woman's voice rang out through the room: "You have to give this food hot to my husband. He has TB."

The door with the double crescents, shut for two hours, opened, and the policemen took the food from the women. They also took the red roses from Kerim's sister.

"Please, do not scream."

"Why shouldn't I? What right do you have to make us wait here for hours?"

The woman yelling is young and strangely beautiful. Her husband is a Communist. A dark young man. And he broke down twice under the sticks. Kerim's sister: "I don't understand Necla. She's a fine, smart woman. How did she fall for that guy and marry him? And she abandoned her family for him. Her father practically disowned her. The police, after all, are scared of her father. The heart, they say, can land on dung or a diamond. I'm not asking why she turned her back on her rich father's house to marry a Communist. But if you're going to marry a Communist, you should marry one like my Kerim. (She smiled, flashing her fine white teeth.) To the raven, her chick is a phoenix."

The women handed over their food. But they stuck around, waiting to take the empty pots back. And something else.

The door with the double crescents opened, and two plain-clothesmen and four detainees walked out. They're carrying baskets for lugging the coal up from the basement to the stoves in the political prisoners' section. Not all the detainees were related to the women outside the door, yet both sides smiled at each other, happy. Necla opened the newspaper before her and pretended to read. One of the prisoners, who knew French, read the headline in *L'Humanité*: "Communists tortured in Turkey. World democrats . . ." He couldn't read any more—the cop next to him gave him a shove: "Move!"

Necla shouted: "Even before my eyes, you're abusing people."

The cop glared at Necla, shook his head, and kept walking. The detainees, lugging the baskets, descended the steps.

Kerim's sister to Neriman: "I hope they don't torture Kerim. I begged so many times to see him just once. But they won't let me."

"I haven't seen Ismail since he went in."

Kerim was in the "coffin." The three walls and the floor of the coffin are cement; the door is wooden. It can fit one man, standing up: back to the wall, knees against the door.

Kerim has spent twenty days in the coffin. They beat him the first day he was arrested, then stuck him in a cell and then the coffin. Overhead burns a light bulb—who knows how many watts—but it glares like crazy. It flickers on and off: now pitch-black, now unbearably bright.

Kerim has spent twenty days in the coffin. For five days they gave him no food. Now they give him a little something. They take him to the bathroom once a day, and he eats his food right there, then back to standing up, now dark, now light.

Kerim has spent twenty days in the coffin. Now they support him under the arms to walk him to the bathroom.

Kerim has spent twenty days in the coffin. He no longer thinks of anything. He has lost the ability to do what they call thinking. And he doesn't feel tired. What he feels is something different from tired. Now dark, now light. At first, he shut his eyes tight, to be free of the now dark, now light. Now he opens and shuts his eyes, opens and shuts them.

On the twenty-sixth night they took Kerim to the bureau chief's office. Ismail was also there. And three faded red roses in a glass on the chief's desk were also there.

The chief, to Ismail: "Do you recognize this man?"

Ismail looked at Kerim's eyes opening and closing. Not just the eyes but his whole face, squinting and relaxing. Then he suddenly knew: the coffin.

"I don't know him."

"He knows you."

"That's a lie."

The bureau chief asks Kerim: "He gave you the typewriter and the stencils, right?"

Kerim is silent. Kerim is not here; he's in another world now totally dark, now madly glaring. His face, his eyes, squint and relax. Two policemen support him under the arms.

Ismail knows: Kerim said nothing at the *falaka* and so ended up in the coffin.

The bureau chief screams at Kerim: "Answer, boy! We know you got it from him. Who'd you give it to?"

Ismail looks into Kerim's eyes. A terrible pain overcomes Ismail. The kid is going crazy.

"Take these bastards down!"

Again, Ismail fought. Kerim just collapsed when he was pushed. They put one foot of each in the same *falaka*. They started with the sticks.

"Take them away."

They took them both back to their cells. Kerim lost his mind ten days later. They took him to the asylum at midnight.

The Twenty-Eighth Line in Izmir

Ismail lit a cigarette with his lighter. Sitting across from him, Ahmet recoiled and pulled back, as if pins had been stuck in his eyes. Ismail put out of his mind the first question that occurred to him. He asked no questions. Ahmet: "It wasn't the lighter, not the flame. I was afraid you'd burn your mustache." But he immediately saw the absurdity of a "burning mustache" and shut up.

They went to bed. Ahmet waited for Ismail to start snoring. He got up, felt around on the table, and found the lighter. He put it up to his face. He waited. He waited a little longer. Then he lit it and felt the flame burn his eyes. He closed his eyes. Then opened and closed them. He opened them and stared at the flame. Am I afraid? He stares at the flame. I'm not afraid, I'm not afraid, I'm not afraid. He closed the lighter and lay back on his bed, lighter in hand. He waited. He flicked it back on. He closed his eyes in fear. I'm afraid. He closed the lighter. Okay, it started here with the fear of fire. But I'm not afraid of water. Which fear comes first? I should read the book. The book is on the table. How can I read it in the dark? He got up. The book fell open to those pages. He lit the lighter without looking at the flame, and turned the barely lit pages of the book. It doesn't say what starts first. Damn it. He put the book back and shut the lighter. He lay down. Not the time for the sleeping pills yet. I can wait two or three more days. Two, three more days. So that's it: I have two, three more days. After two or three more days, once upon a time there was Comrade Ahmet. I choke on the self-pity I've felt these last few days.

THE FOURTEENTH LINE IN ANUSHKA'S DACHA

I DRAW the fourteenth line. Anushka is by my side. We have six days left here. Then Moscow, then a week or ten days, and then Istanbul.

I turn to Anushka: "Give me your hand."

I hold her plump, white hand. Separation is in our clinging palms, but she doesn't know it.

"Ahmet, we'll be late. Let's stop by Petya's on the way back—is he sick or what?" Petya hasn't delivered milk for two days.

"Okay."

At the station, the Nepmen stroll on the high platform, all dressed up. The dachas of Eastern Workers' University are also in our forest. Some of the Eastern students—Chinese, Japanese, Iranian—also promenade on the platform. The priest's daughter is there, too. She and the Iranian Hüseyinzade get along. They walk side by side. None of us Turks are here. There are many peasants with their packs and bundles. And a few *bezprizorni*, the homeless children.

Marusa and Kerim stepped off the train. We hugged. Marusa wore a red scarf and an old leather jacket.

"Marusa," I said, "in ten years, a hundred years, they'll paint your picture like this. The 'Komsomol girl' will appear in movies, plays, and novels, dressed just like you—a *thousand* years from now!"

Marusa was pretty, full-bodied, with light-brown hair and hazel eyes.

"It was overcast this morning—that's why I wore the jacket."

"You'll sweat—take it off."

She took it off and draped it over her arm. Her breasts filled out her short-sleeved, cotton print dress.

Kerim to me in Turkish: "You're crazy in love, man, and still you eye other men's women!"

On the way, Marusa told us things were going well at the factory where she worked. We talked about the *bezprizorni* we saw at the station. Unimaginably dirty, covered in unbelievable rags, they reminded me of Anatolian village children, but in the summertime. Marusa told us what Krupskaya had said about this issue, I don't know how many months ago or where. "We're also working on this at the factory."

We reached Petya's village but didn't know which house was his. Most of the huts lining both sides of the road were sagging; no one was outside in the yards. I looked around. I saw a bearded old man in boots in front of a decent hut with carved window frames and a freshly thatched roof.

"Stay here, I'll go ask."

I walked up to the man. "Hello, comrade. I was going to ask where Petya lives, the son of Daria Mihailovna. His father died in the civil war, fighting in the Red Army. He delivers us milk."

The man didn't answer and stared at me for a while: "Are you a Tartar?"

"I'm a Turk, from Turkey—Istanbul."

The man scratched his beard. His eyes hardened: "So you're Turkish. A Turk. What're you doing here?"

"I'm studying. At the university."

"Like the slant-eyed Chinese at the dacha?"

"Yes."

"Are you staying with them at the dacha?"

"No, with a friend."

At this point, Marusa walked up to us.

The man, still glaring, said, "So every morning Petya delivers your milk?"

It hit me that it was strange for him to talk like this.

"Yes, so what?"

"So what? *So what?* Isn't it enough that you eat Russians' bread and drink Russians' milk? What business do you have here? You mouth off about world revolution and sponge off us. Russians don't have enough Russian bread and milk for themselves."

Marusa jumped in: "You pig, you *kulak*, you!"

Marusa and the man launched into a war of words.

"We're going to wipe you parasites out, you *kulaks*!"

The man swore; Marusa kept up with him. Kerim and Anushka walked up to us. Men, peasant women, and children appeared out of nowhere and surrounded us. Some support Marusa, some the village agha. Petya's mother was a sweet peasant woman.

"Petya is sick," she said, and she turned to the agha: "You should be ashamed, Ivan Petrovich. You're envious because we're selling milk. We have a single cow; you have three. May God's earth feed your endless greed. She turned to us: "Petya is sick," she repeated, "and I didn't have time off from work to deliver it myself."

Anushka: "We were worried about Petya. I'll come and get the milk until he gets better."

For some reason, we didn't go see Petya; we forgot about him after all that commotion.

Daria Mihailovna disappeared and returned with milk.

On the way back to the dacha, Kerim asked in Turkish: "Did you tell the girl anything?"

"No. Of course not. Did you?"

"No."

As we approached the dacha, I said: "Anushka, let's take Petya strawberries tomorrow."

"Good idea."

That night, we lit a fire in a forest clearing. To sit around a fire in a Russian forest is not just beautiful; gazing at the burning pine logs, at the flames of the flames, and falling for them, I don't think—and now I'm going to use a strange word, and in Russian, too—I don't think the *romantika* of it can be found in the forests of any other country. I'm holding Anushka's hand; Marusa's head rests on Kerim's knees. A red glow on all our faces. On all four sides of us, pines and beeches recede, blending into the night.

Marusa asked: "Kerimushka, at least this one night, tonight, do you love me very much?"

If Kerim makes a smart-ass comment, if he says, "Not so much," I'm going to smack his head with whatever I can grab with my free hand.

"Very much," he said. "I love you very, very much, Marusa."

He leaned down, lifted the girl's head lying on his knees, and kissed her on the mouth.

Damn it, I think. I look at Anushka, her forehead, hair, mouth, nose, eyes—in twenty days at most, I'll never see her again. We'll die for each other. Even in bed I've never been as close to her as I am tonight. To be this close to someone, to feel someone so close to me—this secure closeness, which brings tears to my eyes—I know I'll never feel it again. I know all this is only *romantika*. For years my life has been *romantika*. Kerim's, too, and the lives of many people I don't know but will come to know, and Suphi's and Petrosian's, Marusa's and Anushka's—all *romantika*. Who knows, maybe torturous, maybe even bloody—but it's the *romantika* of the Red partisan riding his horse at full gallop. Where's the horseman racing? Many times, to his death. But in the name of life—to live a better, more just, fuller, and deeper life!

Kerim sang Turkish folk songs, his voice very sad: "Here, lady, take my dagger, pierce my heart . . . "

His face changes when he sings, and grows more serious. His amber eyes, flickering in the red glow, are like a young wolf's. He's hungry for life, boundless life.

THE TWENTY-NINTH LINE IN IZMIR

THE MOTOR goes *dum-dum-da-dum-dum*. It pounds inside the cottage, in the lamp's light, in the shadows Ismail and I cast on the walls, over my hands shaking on the table. I cannot look at the lamp wick—the blood-red, frighteningly red wick. And Ismail knows it. He's noticed I haven't been able to look at fire for a while. Although he doesn't believe the answer I always give him, he keeps asking the same question: "How do you feel?"

I don't say I'm fine. I say nothing.

"Is your headache bad?"

I don't answer.

"Does the light hurt your eyes?"

So the cat is out of the bag. How did he, how *could* he, ask that so brutally?

I turn my face to the lamp, to the wick. Ismail watches me with a hunter's eyes. I look at the wick. My pupils burn as if stuck with hot pins. I stare at the wick. The pain is unbearable. I stare at the wick. I stare, and suddenly I go blind. Darkness. I mustn't let Ismail know my darkness. If I don't get hold of myself, I'll scream at the top of my lungs. I stand up without touching the table. It's dark, and my eyes burn. It's dark, but flames leap inside my brain. I take a step. I stagger. Ismail screams: "Sit down!"

Ahmet, suddenly defeated, felt around for the chair and sat down.

"Open your eyes, brother!"

Ahmet realized he had closed his eyes unknowingly. He opened them. The lamp stood behind him. So Ismail changed its place. Ismail is standing. I've never seen him like this. He's scared, and he no longer hides that he's scared.

Ahmet wanted to shout, "Don't be afraid, Ismail!" but he couldn't; he said nothing. Ismail's hand is in his jacket pocket. So he has moved the gun from his pants to his jacket. Must be so he can be faster on the draw. Best take those sleeping pills tonight. All of them.

"How do you feel?"

"I'm fine, Ismail. I was dizzy. It's okay now. I'm fine. I'm going to sleep."

He looks at me strangely. I ask: "Aren't you tired?"

"No."

"What're you going to do?"

"I'll read the papers."

Ahmet, his back to the lamp, took off his clothes. He got into bed. I closed my eyes. I opened them. Ismail sits at the table. He pretends to read the paper while watching me. I turn to the wall. For a while I lie like that, then turn over on my right side again. Ismail has changed his place at the table: he's looking at me, eyes fixed on me, watching. I watch him back from where I'm lying, and the lamp doesn't hurt my eyes anymore. Yet, strangely, I hate Ismail, but I can't let on. Instead, I keep opening and closing my eyes. Ismail looks at me. I touch the bottle of sleeping pills under my pillow. Is this guy going to sit like this till morning? I can't take a handful of sleeping pills before his eyes! Damn it. This business must be settled tonight. It has to be finished. I look at the lamp. My eyes don't burn. This business has to be done tonight. Ismail sits at the table, and I want him to sit there and never take his eyes off me till morning.

LINES AT THE ISTANBUL POLICE HEADQUARTERS

THEY TOOK ISMAIL out of his cell to sleep on a cot, no mattress or blanket, in the hallway by the bathrooms. How many months has he been inside? Now he scratches lines on the wall here. No one sits on the chairs anymore. They let some of them go and put others downstairs in the holding tank. And they haven't called Ismail in for questioning since he and Kerim were beaten on the same *falaka*. Any new arrests? He doesn't know. But since he's been on the cot three days now, he thinks he'd have seen people around if there were new arrests.

They sent the dentist Agop down to the holding tank.

For two days Ismail asks Neriman for dry foods. In the room just past his cot, they've placed someone—who?—in starvation. At night, through the gap under the door of the man's cell, Ismail pushes boreks, cheese, and slices of lunchmeat—stuff like that.

A week after he was put on the cot, they woke Ismail—the bureau chief, the commissioner with glasses, and a plainclothesman: "Let's go."

They turned left off the hallway. The commissioner with glasses opened a door. Ismail saw Ziya. In the empty room, before the barred window without glass—with spring rain coming down outside—Ziya stands naked, wearing only his boxers. His arms are cuffed from behind. His feet are also manacled. They've wound a rope under his armpits and tied its ends to the top bar of the very high window. Ziya's abdomen is stretched out and caved in. All his muscles have elongated, as if stretched by the pull of a terrible weight. Ziya stands on tiptoes, his feet bare. If he tries to relax, the ropes cut into his armpits. His upright head is buried between his shoulders. His eyes are wide open. The rain beats on his back.

The bureau chief asked Ismail: "Do you recognize him?"

"I don't."

"Isn't this the guy who gave you the machine and the stencils?"

"No one gave me anything."

The chief walked up to Ziya: "Do you recognize him?"

"Never seen him."

Ziya's voice was the same, soft and deep.

"Didn't you give the waxed . . ."

Ziya interrupted the chief:

"I didn't give anyone any such thing."

The chief didn't swear. He just shook his head of light-brown hair and left.

Ismail returned to his cot. He's thinking: the bastards have crucified Ziya. He felt great pity, something he hadn't felt since he was thrown inside, and he felt like crying. They've crucified Ziya, the way Sultan Murat crucified Bedreddin's Mustafa on a camel. (He had heard this from Ziya.) The bastards. Then his thought took a different direction: Why didn't they do to me what they did to Kerim and Ziya? As the chief said, he knows I got the machine and the stencils from Ziya and gave them to Kerim. Who told them? But they didn't find the stuff with Kerim. That's why all the torture. (Ismail doesn't yet know Kerim went insane.) And they crucified Ziya because he was in charge, and he'd know whom Kerim gave the machine and the stencils. Stencils, and an old typewriter. Sheaves of waxed paper and an old typewriter. The letter "D" sticks . . .

MULTIPLICATION SIGN: X

AHMET STUDIED the glass in his hand. He sipped the water slowly. He put down the glass, walked over to the sink they washed their faces in—Ziya's work—and turned on the faucet of the big tin can again. He turned it off. Yesterday, washing his face, he'd suddenly felt fear at the sound of water. And he didn't drink water yesterday. But this morning he washed his face just fine and drank the water. He can look at water. He put the thermometer under his arm one more time: 98.7. No headache, no muscle pains. He counted the white lines on the door once more: 32. He took the chalk and drew three vertical lines over the thirty-two lines. He looked at it, then drew an X—its four points touching the four corners of the door—over the thirty-two lines. He smiled. Listening to the motor, he started waiting for Ismail.

AT THE EMINÖNÜ
TROLLEY STOP IN ISTANBUL

SPRING RAIN pours down on Istanbul. And it's getting warm now. Neriman waits at the Eminönü trolley stop. She stands under her umbrella. Her belly is big. The trolleys come and go, the ones she's waiting for: the Aksaray trolleys. Neriman hardly notices. She smiles, mumbling to herself. The Aksaray trolleys pass. "I'll see Ismail tomorrow. They said, 'You'll see him tomorrow.' I'll take Emine, too—tomorrow."

Spring rain pours down—on the dome of the New Mosque, the cones of the minarets, the Golden Horn, the fruit sellers. And the Bridge.

Kerim and Ahmet had sold their papers on a rainy day like this, but then it was only sprinkling. At first, Ahmet had been too embarrassed to sell.

Neriman's heart tightened. They told Kerim's sister that Kerim was transferred to the insane asylum. The poor woman collapsed right there, before the door with the double crescents. She had brought four red roses again.

Spring rain comes down on the fishmarket—on Eminönü Square, the clock on the square, the trolley stop, the roofs, and Neriman's umbrella.

The Aksaray trolleys pass by. Neriman feels an unbearable pain. She bites her lips not to scream. Knives pierce her belly, her groin. I'll see Ismail tomorrow. The pains keep coming. She hails a taxi, lucky to find one in such weather.

Three hours later, in the bedroom of the house in Aksaray and with the help of her midwife neighbor, she bore Ismail a girl. The neighbors had called Kadıköy from the market phone and told Osman Bey to come. Osman Bey, holding Emine by the hand, paced up and down outside the bedroom door. So her brother wouldn't hear her scream, so nobody would hear her scream,

Neriman bit her lips into open wounds. The bed sheets were torn. She bore Ismail a girl.

Spring rain falls on Istanbul. On their unpainted wooden house with its latticework balcony, spring rain comes down.

On the Train

As SOON as Ismail stepped in, Ahmet showed him the back of the door: "Look."

Ismail looked. He understood. They hugged.

"I didn't wait for forty or forty-one, Ismail."

"You did right. Anyway . . . (He didn't finish.) I'll go get some rakı, brother."

"Tomorrow I want to go to Balıkesir to see Ziya."

"You know best, but . . ."

"It's too soon to go to Istanbul. I want to talk to Ziya and see how we can make use of this hole. We don't need to bring up this matter at a meeting here. Ziya is the only one in charge who didn't get caught."

Ahmet shaved his mustache. He stuffed cotton inside his upper and lower lips to change the shape of his mouth. And they used iodine to burn a patch above his left eye that looked like a wound.

"Is my face different?"

"Quite."

"Let me see your ID."

The picture on Ismail's ID looks like anyone but him. Ismail has a hat like an American sailor's hat. Ahmet tried it on and combed his hair down on his forehead under the hat.

"Your face has really changed, brother."

The next morning they both woke up early. They hugged. Ismail wasn't going to work: "You can't leave the door open. Who'd you leave the key with?"

At the train station, as Ahmet climbed aboard the third-class car, a man caught his eye. Standing on the platform, the man looks like he's watching everyone get on the train. I think I know this man. Or am I confusing him with someone? Does he look like the man outside the *Aydınlık* offices, keeping tabs on who comes and goes? No, no. I'm being paranoid again, damn it.

The train started. Ahmet rested his head against the window next to him.

Anushka rests her head on the glass of the rail car. We're returning to Moscow, hand in hand. Forests pass outside. We don't talk. She clutches my hand, as if I'll leave her there and run away. I'm mumbling: "Listen to the flute's lament, it grieves its separation."

"Are you reciting your mystic poet's lines, again?"

"How'd you know?"

"Their rhythm. Say them again, first in Turkish and then in Russian. But whisper them in my ear."

I say the lines.

"It's very sad. This flute you call a *ney*—do they have them in the Caucasus, in Central Asia?"

"Probably. What would you do with it?"

"I'll try to find one. I couldn't play it, but I could hang it in my room."

The man I saw on the platform entered the compartment. He sat across from me. He really looks a lot like the other guy. Damn it. He tries not to look at me, almost forcing himself. Well, if they're following me, they won't arrest me right away. They want to see my contact. Should I meet Ziya or not? I shouldn't bring trouble down on his head. The man stepped outside. We're nearing a station, and the train is slowing down. So this guy is not that man—see, he's getting off here.

I looked out the window to see if he got off, but I couldn't tell. But if he got off the other side, I wouldn't see him anyway.

The train started.

Anushka holds my hand tight. Beech trees speed past. Russians love beeches. What trees do we love? Poplars? Plane trees? What trees do I love? Willows? But they're always weeping.

I . . . *Anushka! Anushka!* The *Anushka's* I thought I was saying to myself I had said out loud.

"What is it, Ahmedushka?"

"I'll never love anyone as much as I love you."

"In a couple of years, Ahmedushka, you'll go back home to your country. You'll remember me for a while. Sure, you'll remember me, but then . . . But that's not what matters. We still have a year or two. Let's think of these years."

My insides knotted. Even if I wanted to say I'd be gone in a week or ten days, tops, I knew I couldn't. The last night, maybe. And the day after I disappear, Anushka will understand anyway. So what would it hurt to tell her a day ahead? I cannot conceive how I'd tell Anushka. I must get this thing off my mind right now—do something! My eye caught the package Anushka had wrapped in old newspapers. I read the headlines: "Terror in Romania. Fifth Year of the Comintern."

I saw that man again in the corridor. I mean, he glanced into my compartment and pulled back his head. Clearly, they recognized me as I was getting on the train. How can I get off at one of the upcoming stations without being seen? I have to give up on going to Ziya. So where should I go? My ticket is up to Balıkesir.

We're nearing Moscow. Anushka: "Kerim and Marusa will meet us at the station, right?"

"So they said."

"Kerim is a really good man. The more people like him you have in your party, the better the work you can do."

The newspaper catches my eye again. I read the same news: "Terror in Romania, Fifth Year of the Comintern."

We pass through the Moscow suburbs, Anushka's hand in mine.

We pass some foothills. The man sits across from me, dozing. Is he really dozing or just pretending?

My Guests

I HAVE GUESTS: Anushka, Ismail, Ahmet, Neriman, Marusa, Ziya, Si-Ya-U.

Kerim's not here. He died. Not in the asylum. He recovered and got out. He died of TB in May of 1950.

My guests haven't aged. They're still the age they were when I last saw them. Si-Ya-U is still in love with Anushka; Ahmet is still jealous of Si-Ya-U.

Ziya: "Read me a poem."

I read:

> I'm a worker,
>> love from head to toe:
>> love sees, thinks, and understands,
>> love is a newborn advancing light,
>> love hitches a swing to the stars,
>> love casts steel in a sweat.
>
> I'm a worker,
>> love from head to toe.

I translated the poem into Russian for Marusa and Anushka. Ismail lit his cigarette from mine.

"You wrote that good," he said. Then he stood up, opened the window, and let sunlight into the room.

Ahmet's hand holds Anushka's plump white hand and long fingers.

Neriman repeated her husband's words in her deep voice: "Life's good, brother."

My guests haven't aged. They're still the age they were when I last saw them, but I'm past sixty. If I could just live five more years . . .

THE END

Glossary

AHI BROTHERHOOD: Thirteenth-century Muslim community established by Ahi (1169–1261) in Kayseri.

ARUZ: Quantitative meters imported from Arabic and Persian verse that were adopted as the basis for Ottoman court poetry.

AVEROF: Greek battleship.

BARBAROS HAYRETTIN: Khayr ad-Din, Barbary pirate and later admiral in command of the Ottoman fleet that annexed Algeria and Tunisia into the Ottoman Empire.

BÖRKLÜCE MUSTAFA: Follower of Sheik Bedreddin, who led a brutally crushed peasant rebellion against Sultan Murat. Nâzım tells this story in "The Epic of Sheik Bedreddin."

CEBESOY, ALI FUAT (1882–1968): Nâzım's uncle in Ankara, Atatürk's closest friend since military school, and one of the generals who helped found the Turkish Republic.

CUP: Committee of Union and Progress, known in the West as the Young Turks.

DENIKIN: A general in the White Army during the Russian Civil War.

INDEPENDENCE TRIBUNALS: Revolutionary courts that exercised broad powers through the early twenties.

ISMET PASHA: Inönü, Independence War hero and second president of Turkey (1938–1950).

KAZIM KARABEKIR PASHA (1882–1948): Turkish general active in shaping the Turkish Republic.

KING KONSTANTIN (1868–1923): Reigning monarch during the Greek invasion of Turkey and the ensuing Independence War.

KOLCHAK, ALEKSANDR VASILIYEVICH: The naval commander who led the anti-Bolshevik forces during the Russian Civil War.

LAZ: An ethnic group that settled on the Black Sea coast of Turkey.

NEPMEN: Soviet entrepreneurs allowed by Lenin's New Economic Policy (NEP).

"LAME" OSMAN: Atatürk's famed bodyguard from the Black Sea region.

ROBERT COLLEGE: An American-style university, with instruction in English, founded in 1863.

SULTANAHMET PRISON: The Istanbul Detention House, built in 1918–19.

SUPHI, MUSTAFA: Founder of the first Turkish Communist Party in Baku, Azerbaijan (1920).

SYLLABICS: The measure of Turkish folk poetry, governed by the number and pattern of syllables.

TASHNAK: Armenian Revolutionary Federation, a political party founded in Tbilisi in 1890.

About the Author

NÂZIM HIKMET was born in 1902 in Salonika, then part of the Ottoman Empire, and grew up in Istanbul, where he lived through the First World War and the end of the Empire. Escaping occupied Istanbul in 1921, he traveled through a backward and poverty-stricken Anatolia during the Turkish War of Independence and witnessed the formation and early years of the Turkish Republic in Ankara. His experiences in Turkey and his subsequent years as a student in Moscow in the twenties radicalized him and determined the course of his life and work. Returning to Turkey, he endured years of persecution and imprisonment for his writings, which freely expressed his Communist beliefs, and he eventually served a thirteen-year sentence between 1938 and 1950. Released in an amnesty in 1950, continuing persecution by the Turkish authorities drove him into exile in Moscow the following year. In the Soviet Union he experienced communism in practice. Having lost his Turkish citizenship, he could never go back to Turkey and died in exile in 1963.

Although Hikmet's work was banned in Turkey for thirty years, today he is recognized as the first and foremost modern Turkish poet. His work has been translated into more than fifty languages around the world, and he is internationally acclaimed as one of the greatest poets of the twentieth century.

A full account of Hikmet and the history he lived through, his poetry and politics, and the women he loved can be found in *Nâzım Hikmet: The Life and Times of Turkey's World Poet,* by Mutlu Konuk Blasing.